I0663344

An Original Screenplay

by

Ron Sellz

LOST AGE PUBLISHING
—2017—

Hollywood Friends © 2017 Ron Sellz

An Original Screenplay by Ron Sellz

All rights reserved. No part of this book may be reproduced or transmitted in any form or by any means, electronic or mechanical, including photocopying, recording, or by any information storage and retrieval system, without permission in writing from the Author.

The following original screenplay has been filed and registered with the Writers' Guild of America, West, under the name of Ron Sellz.

Printed in the United States of America

Cover art and interior design by: Cyrusfiction Productions.

First Edition Paperback
ISBN: 978-1-946480-16-3

9018 Balboa Boulevard
Suite #562
Northridge, CA 91325

BOUND 4 VEGAS

WRITTEN BY

RON SELLZ

WGAw ®

Written by Ron Sellz

BOUND 4 VEGAS

FADE IN

EXT. MIDDLE CLASS HOME - DAY - PAN THE AREA

The home is a ranch style house. The grounds are neatly
manicured, along with nicely placed bushes along the walkway
to the front door

SHOOT THRU TO:

INT. HOUSE - CONTINUING - WE HEAR A LOT OF MALE VOICES
COMING FROM THE DINING ROOM.

A card game is going on. The boys are all in their twenties.
Gary and a girl are in the bathroom which is a few feet away
from the card table.

                    JEFF
               (YELLS TOWARDS BATHROOM)
          You guys are sick ... Why don't
          you get a room?

                    RICK
               (butting in)
          He gave me twenty bucks for the
          bathroom rights.

                    GARY (V.O.)
               (from inside the bathroom)
          Rooms cost too much.

                    JEFF
          What are the rest of us supposed
          to do? We need to use the
          bathrooms too you know.

                    GARY (V.O.)
               (annoyed)
          So hold it! Use Rick's parents'.

                    RICK
          Sorry Jeff. Their room is off
          limits.

Jeff has the cards in his hands. He yells toward, the
bathroom.

>   JEFF
>   We're dealing you out Gary

>   GARY (V.O.)
>   (Yelling back at Jeff)
>   If you were a-good friend, you'd
>   wait a few seconds.

>   JEFF
>   We're not good friends. I'm
>   dealing you out.

Jeff deals out the cards. They check their hands. Jeff puts
his chips on his cards. Rick sits quietly with his cards on
the table. This bothers Jeff.

>   JEFF
>   What's with you Rick? You're like
>   "silent Sam" over there. Why
>   don't we kick Gary out of the
>   game?

>   GARY (V.0)
>   (Yelling)
>   Just cause you' re dealing, that
>   doesn't mean you get to call the
>   shots. It's Rick's house jackass!

>   JEFF
>   If he were winning, I'd kick him
>   out, but he's losing.

Mark and Rick lose. Jeff takes the pot, and gets ready to
deal another hand.

>   JEFF (CONT'D)
>   No cards to anyone not in a seat.

FULL SHOT - THE BATHROOM OPENS AND GARY AND CONNIE EXIT.
GARY TUCKS IN HIS SHIRT HALFWAY. GARY IS A GOOD-LOOKING SLOB
IN HIS EARLY 20'S.

> GARY (TO CONNIE)
> I'm in. Sorry you have to split.

Then, Gary takes an open seat at the table. He is passed over and doesn't get any cards.

> GARY (CONT'D)
> What about me?

> JEFF
>
> Sorry. You're too late. I'll put
> you in next hand.

> GARY (PISSED)
> That's bullshit!

Then, Mark writes something on a piece of paper and puts it into the pot. Rick picks up the paper and looks at it. He then tosses it back into the pot.

> RICK (DISGUSTED)
> Another I.O.U.?

> MARK
> My money's good. I get paid
> Monday.

> JEFF
> I don't even know why we even let
> you play. You never show up with
> money and you always have some
> story about why you can't pay
> what you owe.

> MARK
> Weekends are tough. You know
> that.

> JEFF
> So is life. (A BEAT) Who's up?

> RICK
> Hit! me.

Jeff deals a card to Rick. shuffles them. He waits. Rick picks up his cards and He takes too long.

                    JEFF
          Sometime today Rick.

                    MARK
          Yeah man, let's go.

                    RICK
               (Friendly)
          I'm good jackass.

                    JEFF

          Well?

Mark and Rick expose their cards. They have eighteen. Jeff
has seventeen. They beat Jeff's hand. Then, Jeff pays them off
and gathers up the cards. He then hands them to Rick.

                    JEFF (CONT'D)
          Your deal.

Rick takes the cards and begins to shuffle the deck.
                    RICK
          Okay. Same game.

Rick deals out the hands. (beat) They all look over their
cards.

                    GARY
          I'm good.

WE SEE that he has twenty. He fidgets with his gold chains.

                    RICK
          We're not here so you could screw
          some skank! We came to play
          cards.

                    GARY
          Screw you guys. You're all jealous.

                    RICK
          Shut up and play cards or would you
          prefer we play in the bathroom?

EVERYONE LAUGHS

                    GARY
        Not funny Rick.

                    MARK
        I think he's damn funny.

                    GARY
        Sorry, I can't hear a guy who
        plays with I.O.U.'s.

Mark writes out something-on a piece of paper and slides it
to Gary. Gary reads it aloud.

                    GARY (CONT'D)
        Fuck off!

                    JEFF
        That's mature.

                    RICK
        Let's just play.

Rick deals out the cards. They look at their cards. Then;

                    MARK
        Check.
                    JEFF
        Check.
                    RICK
        I'll check.

Gary throws twenty dollars into the pot.

                    GARY
        I'm in for twenty smackers.

                    MARK
        Why can't you just check?

                    RICK
        Damn it Gary. It's our first damn
        hand. Can't you just go slow?

                         GARY
                    (Pleased with himself)
          Maybe you guys need to learn
          how to play the game. (beat)
          Listen. A guy goes to a butcher
          and says I'll take the steak.
          (Remembering) Oh shit! Never
          mind. That's the punch line.

Rick picks up his chips and throws them into the pot.

                         RICK
          Can't you even tell a joke?
          (beat) Just for that, I'll raise
          you twenty.

                         MARK
          I'm out

Mark throws in his cards.

                         JEFF

          I'm good. You need joke lessons.
          Gary

Jeff puts in some chips with one hand and adds a few more
chips with the other. Then, he throws in five more.

Gary's chips are stacked against the edge of the table. His
belly presses against the table ... He matches Jeff's bet.

                         RICK
              Cards?

                         JEFF
          Give me three please.

Rick deals three and takes back the three he didn't want.

                         GARY
                    (confidently)
          I'm good. I'll play these.

Rick pulls two cards out of his hand and tosses them into
the discard pile. He takes two. Rick deals himself two fresh

cards and looks at his hand. Then, he stares at Gary for a few moments. Jeff also stares at Gary. And stares ...

>   RICK
>   It's to you Jeff

>   JEFF
>   Good.

>   RICK
>   I guess I'm good too.

Now, it's Gary's turn. He slams down some chips.

>   GARY
>   Forty more!

Rick and Jeff stare at the chips against Gary's stomach.

>   GARY (CONT'D)
>   Now you guys know that the losers
>   have to pay the winner, right?

>   JEFF
>   We know ... Quit stalling

Rick and Jeff stare at Gary's chips. They are shaking.

>   MARK
>   Can I get back into the game?

They ignore Mark.

>   GARY
>   (nervous)
>   This is just a hand of poker.

>   RICK
>   Yep! That sure is a lot of money

Suddenly, Gary's stack of chips falls over. Now, Jeff and Rick are ready to make their move and pounce on him.

>   JEFF
>   I'll see your forty and raise
>   fifty.

Jeff pushes more chips into the pot.

> RICK
> Yeah, me to. And add fifty.

Rick pushes in more chips. Now, it's up to Gary. He pushes a pile of chips into the pot. Rick leans over and counts Gary's chips.

> RICK (CONT'D)
> All right Gary. Your twenty short.

> GARY
> (acting surprised)
> Whoops. Sorry about that.

Gary throws in more chips into the pot.

> RICK
> Okay Gary. Let's see 'em.

Gary flips over his cards and shows everyone that he tried to bluff. He is visibly shaken. He has nothing.

> GARY
> I've got shit! God damn it! How come whenever I'm bluffing you guys always know? All the damn time.

> RICK
> Cause Gary. You're so god-damn fat, your stomach starts to shake and when your chips fall over, we know you're bluffing.

Rick and Jeff divide their winnings. Gary is pissed.

> GARY
> Damn it you guys. You're cheaters.

> JEFF
> How is that cheating? You've got a tell. We can't help it if your stomach shakes like jello and we didn't have to tell you either.

                    GARY
          (to Rick)
You're a lawyer. Can you legally
use a person's stomach against
him?

                    RICK
You can figure that one out.

                    MARK
          (getting up)
I'm leaving guys.

                    GARY
Did you run out of I.O.U.'s?

                    MARK
Screw you Gary. Everybody gets
paid on Monday except you. You
owe me.

               MARK (CONT'D)
          (heading for the door)
Later guys. And screw you Gary.

                    JEFF
Bye Mark.

                    RICK
See ya.

                                        Mark exits

                    GARY
I'm glad he's gone. How can I
owe a guy money who plays with
I.O.U.'s?

                    RICK
It's a shitty way to play.

                    JEFF
Yeah. It is pretty low. (beat)
Forget about him. Let's eat.

                    RICK
It's after twelve. No one's open.

                 GARY
Pizza Joe's. The restaurant's
closed, but they deliver till
two.

                 JEFF
What do you say we order a bunch
of food and beer for the house
down the street and take the stuff
from the truck when he's at the
other house?
                 GARY
What if we're caught?

Gary turns on the television.

                 RICK
Easy. If he sees us, we' 11
run away in three different
directions. He'll never catch us.
It's a perfect plan.

Jeff picks up his I-Phone and punches in a phone number.

                 JEFF
Hi. Is this the pizza place? ...

Gary and Rick sit back at the poker table. Rick picks up the
cards, then playfully smacks Gary's hand.

                 RICK
How about a little blackjack?

                 GARY
I'll only play if you don't stare
at my stomach or my chips.

                                 CUT TO:

DINING ROOM - Rick returns with a few black shirts. He
throws them onto the couch.

                 RICK
Grab a shirt and put it on.

                         GARY
          Don't you have any other colors?

                         JEFF
          Gary, the idea is to wear black
          so we don't stand out in the
          dark.

                         GARY
          Ohhhhhh ... Hey, where'd you get
          all these black shirts?

                         RICK
          They're my sisters. She's messed
          up.

Everyone puts on their shirt. Gary's stomach sticks out of
his. He looks ridiculous. It's too small. Gary's not happy.

                         GARY
          I can't wear this shirt

                         RICK
          C'mon Gary. Be a team player.
          It's just for a little bit.

                         JEFF
          I feel like this is, "Mission
          Impossible".

                         RICK
                (heading for the door)
          Follow me outside and don't make
          a lot of noise. These pizza
          guys are fast, so we have to be
          faster.

EXT. RICKS HOUSE - MINUTES LATER - CONTINUING

Rick and company head down the walkway. There are trash cans
up and down the street. Gary hides behind two cans as Rick
and Jeff approach.

                         JEFF
          Who are you hiding from?

GARY

Shut up! I know what I'm doing.

RICK

Yes sir. (turns to Jeff) What a
dumb-ass!!!

Jeff heads down the street. He points to a house on the other
side of the street. The walkway has a lot of bushes on it
and the front doors porch has even more growth around it.
Jeff and Rick run over to Gary. They're winded.

JEFF

Here's the plan. Gary hides
behind the trash cans across from
their house. If you see the pizza
truck guy coming back while we're
in his truck, give us the head's
up.

GARY

You mean signals like animal
noises?

RICK

Seriously? Can do animals sounds?

GARY

Sure. A Rhesus monkey or a sloth.

JEFF

(aghast)
What the hell does a Rhesus
monkey sound like?

RICK

(interrupting)
Forget about it Jeff. And Gary,
you shut the hell up. Who the
hell ever heard of a Rhesus
monkey alarm?

GARY

Another monkey ...

                    JEFF
          Look Gary, just stay behind the
          trash cans and drop the lid on
          the ground ... (beat) That's the
          alarm. Rick and I will grab as
          much stuff as we can and get back
          to the house.

                                        DISSOLVE TO:

EXT. RICK'S HOUSE -MINUTES LATER

A pizza truck drives up the street. There is a lit "Pizza
sign" on the top of the truck. The truck parks in the
driveway of the house. Then, the driver takes out a pizza
and leaves the truck. The driver heads for the door.

WIDE SHOT ON TRUCK - RICK AND JEFF RUN OVER TO THE TRUCK.

Rick jumps inside and hands Jeff a bunch of stuff until his
arms are full.

                    JEFF
          I'm full.

Rick exits the truck and puts the stuff on the seat

                                        CUT TO:

EXT. FRONT DOOR OF CUSTOMER'S HOUSE - CONTINUING

The driver knocks on the door but, no one answers.

                                        CUT TO:

EXT. PIZZA TRUCK - CONTINUING

As Rick and Jeff are ready to leave, Gary appears.

                    GARY
          How's it going guys?

                    RICK
               (surprised)
          What the hell are you doing here?

                    JEFF
Didn't we tell you to look
out and warn us if something
happened?

                    GARY
Yeah, but I'm bored. (beat) Can
I have a piece of mushroom or
pepperoni pizza or something?

                    RICK
You idiot! Are you nuts? You're
the lookout!!!

                                        CUT TO:

The pizza person appears. First, Gary is spotted on the side
of the truck. Seeing this, Gary grabs the top of a nearby
trash can lid and drops it on the ground.

                    GARY
         Run!!!

Our guys scatter. Gary runs away while trying to hold up his
pants. Then, as if from out of nowhere, the pizza person
trips Gary as he passes a corner. Gary lets out a scream,
and tries to keep his pants on while being sat on by the
pizza employee. Then, the pizza guy takes his hat off and we
see that he is a she. A pizza girl.

                    PIZZA GIRL
You're in a lot of trouble, fat
boy!
                    GARY
You would never have caught me if
I didn't trip.

                    PIZZA GIRL
I was the one who tripped you.
You're going to jail.

                    GARY
         Jail???

                    PIZZA GIRL
You and your friends robbed me.

She takes out her cell phone and punches in a number.

                    PIZZA GIRL
          Hello 911?

                    GARY
          But, I was just jogging by. I
          don't even know Jeff and Rick.

The Pizza Girl stares at Gary.

                                        CUT TO:

INT. RICK'S HOUSE - MINUTES LATER

Jeff and Rick sit down after piling their loot on the table.

                    RICK
          Gary's busted for sure.

                    JEFF
          He's gonna need a good lawyer.
          (beat) Are you any good?

ANGLE ON FRONT DOOR - GARY WALKS IN LIKE NOTHING'S HAPPENED.

                    JEFF
          What happened to you?

                    RICK
          You were busted. I know you.

                    GARY
          Who me? Are you kidding.

                    JEFF
          C'mon Gary. What really happened?

                    GARY
          I gave him a hundred bucks and he
          let me go.

Rick shakes his head.

                    RICK
        It was probably a girl. We could
        have bought this stuff for less.

                    JEFF
        Even delivered.

Gary walks over to the table and grabs some pizza. Then, he
turns on the television.

FULL ANGLE ON TELEVISION - IT'S A REPORT ON LAS VEGAS

                    T. V. REPORTER
        And so, like so many hotels
        before it, The Desert Sands will
        become a distant memory. It was
        one of Elvis Presley's favorite
        haunts. And now, this appears.to
        be the last diamond on the strip.
        (beat) For KLAS, this is David
        Scott.

                    JEFF
            (excited)
        How 'bout we go there one last
        time?

                    RICK
        You only liked it because Gary's
        dad always got us the V.I.P.
        treatment.

                    JEFF
        What do you say Gary? When will
        you finally admit that you father
        is mobbed up?

                    GARY (JOKINGLY)
        If I did, I 'd have to kill you
        all.

                    JEFF
        Do you think you can talk to your
        dad and get us a big suite and
        shit?

>   GARY
> It would really suck if we
> weren't there for the end.

>   RICK
> We could have a total blowout.
> (beat) C'mon Gary. Give old dad a
> call.

>   GARY
> (Thinking, then) What the hell.
> I'll bug him until he says yes.

THE FRONT DOOR OPENS AND RICK'S FAMILY ENTERS.

Ricks parents are attractive. Joe and Mary. His mother
doesn't have to wear as much make-up as she does. Anyone who
kisses her comes away with a splotch on their face. Rick's
younger cousin Connie is ten years younger than he is. She's
not interested in Rick or his friends.

All the women retire into the kitchen, but Rick's father
stays with the guys.

>   JOE
> So, what's going on with you
> guys?

>   RICK
> Have some pizza dad.

>   GARY
> We were talking about going to
> Vegas.

>   JOE
> I wish I could be there with you.
> (beat) you staying at the Sands?

>   JEFF
> We've got to go before it closes.
> It's always been a cool hotel.
> It's like stepping back in time.

>   JOE
> I wish I could go with you.

                         RICK
          Maybe Gary's dad can get you a
          room.

                         JOE
          Is your dad really connected?

                         GARY
                       (pissed)
          You guys are a bunch of assholes!
          ... Not you Joe.

The kitchen door opens. Joe's wife steps into the room.

                         MARY
          Joe, honey. I have enough for us and
          the boys, but no dessert. We need an
          ice cream cake from the store.

                         JOE
          You hear your mother?

Joe takes some money out of his pocket and puts it into
Rick's hand. Rick takes it then, Rick hands the money to Jeff
and he and Gary head for the door

                         RICK
          I'm gonna hang back here. It
          doesn't take three guys to buy an
          ice cream cake.

Jeff and Gary exit.

                                              CUT TO:

EXT. HOUSE

Gary and Jeff bundle up as the wind picks up.

Jeff gets into Gary's customized Honda Accord.

                         JEFF
          Whoever did the work on this car,
          cut a lot of corners on it.

Jeff has to slam the door a few times to get it to close.

DISSOLVE TO:

INT. RICK'S HOUSE - MINUTES LATER

Everyone's in the living room. The television's on.

                         JOE
                    (to Rick)
          So, do you have a plan for Vegas?

                         RICK
          I'm sure the three of us will
          stay busy. Don't worry.

                         JOE
          How about "hookers?" I'll bet
          your friends really like them.

                         MARY
          All this talk about hookers and
          things. Why don't you take some
          of the nice girls you know?

                         JOE
                    (interrupting)
          No honey. It's gonna be a sausage
          fest.

                         MARY
                    (perplexed)
          A what?

                         RICK
          It's just the three of us, mom.

EXT HOUSE - NIGHT - MINUTES LATER

It's starting raining as Gary's car comes up the street and
does a U-turn in front of Rick's house. It ends up parked in
front. Then, it begins pouring.

INT. HONDA

Gary and Jeff sit in the car as the rain comes down. They are clearly not prepared for this weather. Gary leans across to Jeff's side and rolls down his window.

                    JEFF.
          Are you crazy.
Gary sticks his head out of Jeff's window and yells.

                    GARY
          Help, help, help!!!

                    JEFF
          What are you doing yelling
          "help"?

                    GARY
          If I yell rain, do you think
          anyone is gonna come?

Suddenly, the rain stops.

                    JEFF
          Let's head in before it starts.
          (then) Hand me the bag.

In the back seat is a bag containing the ice cream cake. Gary gets it. Then, Rick opens the passenger door and we notice the gutter of rushing water. There's all types of debris mixed in the gutter water. It looks rather gross.

Gary hands the bag to Jeff at an awkward angle.

CLOSE SHOT - JEFF TAKES THE BAG WITH TWO FINGERS

                    GARY
          Watch out dude. (then)

                    JEFF
          No! Don't hand me the bag like
          that... Shit!!!

ANGLE - ON ICE CREAM CAKE FROM OUTSIDE LOOKING IN

Suddenly, from out of the bag slips the box containing the ice cream cake. Gary reaches over and catches the box, but the ice cream cake falls out of the box and into the gutter.

WIDE SHOT - ON GUTTER AND ICE CREAM CAKE, AS THE RAIN WATER
AND EVERYTHING ELSE FLOWS OVER THEIR DIRTY DESSERT.

> GARY
>> (panicked)
> What'll we do?

> JEFF
> This.

WIDE ANGLE ON SIDE OF CAR AND GUTTER

Jeff's hands reach out and scoops up the gooey mess. He
manages to push the smaller cake back into the box. He
reaches in to pinch off a couple of leafs.

> JEFF (CONT'D}
> This is really gross.

> GARY
> Now what?

Jeff closes up he box and puts it back into the bag.

> JEFF
> Just do what I do and keep that
> mouth of yours shut. I mean it
> Gary!

> GARY
> Count on me. But, do you think I
> could just have a little piece?

> JEFF
> No, you idiot. It's gutter cake.

> GARY
> Oh yeah ...

Jeff exits the car carrying the bag. Gary follows.

INT. RICK'S HOUSE - CONTINUING

Everyone is seated as Jeff and Gary enter the room carrying
the bag. Mary takes it from Jeff.

                    MARY
         I hope it's good. We're starving.

Jeff takes a seat next to Rick. Then, he drops his fork. As
Rick reaches down for it, Jeff bends down too.

LOW SHOT:

                    JEFF
         Don't eat the ice cream cake. It
         was in the gutter. It's shit!

                    RICK
         No shit?

                    JEFF
         You'd better tell your parents

Mary brings the cake to the table and everyone except our
trio has a piece.

                    RICK
         It's probably better that what my
         mom usually cooks.

Gary pokes Rick.

                    GARY
         How much do you like your cousin?

                    RICK
         Let her eat it. She's a bitch.

Joe likes it and takes a second helping.

                    JOE
         This is great stuff.

                    MARY
         What's the matter with you boys?

Mary puts a plate of ice cream in front of Gary.

                    JOE
         Eat up son.

Gary looks all around nervously. Then, he picks up a fork. He takes a little piece. As his hand moves towards his mouth,
his hand begins shaking. It shakes so much that as it inches closer, it falls off his fork.

CLOSE ANGLE ON CONNIE - SHE BITES INTO A ROCK

                    CONNIE
          Ouch!!!

                    MARY
          What's the matter honey?

Connie pulls a pebble out of her mouth.

                    CONNIE
          I think I bit into a rock.

                    JEFF
          No, no, no. It's probably a nut.

                    GARY
          Yeah, a nut.

                    JEFF
          They had two ice cream cakes.
          One was regular and the other
          one was called, "Ice cream cake
          surprise". I guess we got the nut
          surprise.

                    MARY
          Ouch!!! I just got another
          surprise

Mary spits a rock onto her plate. Connie spits too.

RICK COAXES JEFF AND GARY TO GET UP AND HEAD FOR THE DOOR

                    JOE
          What's the hurry boys?
               (Joe spits another pebble.)
          I was gonna ask you boys to fetch
          us another delicious ice cream
          cake.

                         RICK
          I'm afraid that was the last one.
          But, I'11 be back later before we
          go to Vegas.

                                          THEY EXIT
Everyone continues eating and spitting. Connie starts
coughing and pulls a leaf from her mouth.

                         MARY
          Aren't you lucky. That's probably
          a bay leaf. I wish I got one.

               JOE - MARY - CONNIE
          OUCH!!!

                                       DISSOLVE TO:

EXT. LARGE MANSION SATURDAY MORNING

The air is still as an SUV pulls up to the house. Rick and
Jeff jump out of the car and run up the driveway past several
fancy cars. Gary's car is the only plain one.

                                          CUT TO:

INT. GARY'S BEDROOM - MOMENTS LATER

Gary is sprawled out across his bed. He is asleep.

SFX: ALARM - IT CONTINUES TO BEEP IN A VERY ANNOYING MANNER.

Gary reaches out and swipes the radio off it's stand.

                         GARY
          Shut the hell up, god damn it! !!

SFX - KNOCKING AT HIS DOOR CUT TO:

Rick and Jeff are outside Gary's bedroom door. Jeff tries
yelling through the door.

                         JEFF
          Open up Gary!

                    RICK
               (yelling)
          Time to go!

RICK AND JEFF KICK AND POUND ON THE DOOR.

INT. GARY'S ROOM - ANGLE ON GARY IN HIS BED

Gary opens his eyes. He is very restless and very annoyed.

                    GARY
               (loudly)
          Go away. (beat) I'm sleeping!

                    JEFF (yelling)
          Wake the hell up Gary. We're
          going to Vegas.

THE KICKING AND POUNDING ON GARY'S DOOR CONTINUES.

                                        CUT TO:

                    JEFF & RICK
               (yelling)
          GET UP!!!

                    GARY (V.O.)
          Come back later.

                    RICK
          Hey Gary ... We've got donuts.

Suddenly, the door opens. Gary's bathrobe is half open.

Rick and Jeff ignore Gary and walk into his room. Jeff takes
his spot on the easy chair while Rick lies down on Gary's
other bed. Gary slams the door and flops down on his bed. He
almost gets lost in the pile of clothes on his bed.

                    GARY
          You jerks tricked me. There's no
          donuts.

                    RICK
          Let's get the hell on the road.

                    GARY
          I'm ready to go. I just need a
          couple of things.

                    JEFF
          You mean like clean clothes?

                    GARY
          Do I go to your place and bitch?

                    JEFF
          You never come to my house.

                    RICK
          How long's it gonna take you to
          pack and be ready?

Gary points to some bags by the door. He finally gets up.

EXT. AERIAL SHOT OF GARY'S HOUSE - MINUTES LATER

We see Gary's Honda backing out of the driveway. He's even
speeding in reverse and almost hits a car that's going in
the opposite direction. Then, he speeds away and hits his
own mail box and knocks it down.

                                        DISSOLVE TO:

EXT. GAS STATION AND MINI MART - MINUTES LATER

The Honda sits at the pump. It's ready to go.

INT. HONDA - CONTINUING

                    GARY
          Okay guys. Pony up some money.

                    RICK
          I don't think so man. You' re
          just gonna pocket it

                    GARY
          No I won't.

                    JEFF
          We know it's going on daddy's card.

                    GARY
          It's part of my allowance. I have
          to pay him back.

                    RICK
          Since when. He's your ATM.

Jeff opens up a bag of goodies from the mini mart.

                    GARY
          Give me an extra-large anything
          to drink. I'm dying of thirst. I
          need liquids before I faint.

Jeff hands the bag to Rick who takes out some Twinkies. Gary
grabs a large drink out of the bag.

                    GARY
          Thanks man. I mean Rick. Not you,
          Jeff.

                    JEFF
          What are you talking about. I was
          the one who pumped the gas.

                                        CUT TO:

They drive away from the gas station and onto the freeway

                                        DISSOLVE TO:

INT. CAR - TWO HOURS LATER -

Rick wakes up and decides that everyone should be up. Gary
continues to drive.

                    RICK
          Wake up guys. We gotta be close
          to Zzyzx road or something.

                    JEFF
          How the hell do you spell it?

                    GARY
          Z-y-s-s-y-x is how. And it's
          exactly one hundred miles from

Vegas. Besides, I just saw a
sign. It said, one mile ahead.

                    JEFF
Who cares how it's spelled as
long as we get there. And by the
way, you screwed up the spelling.

                    GARY
Bullshit! I spelled it right.
Anyway, I just remembered a joke
I made up.

                    JEFF
Give us a break.

                    GARY
No. You'll really like it. You
see this guy was walking down
the street with a parrot on his
shoulder and the parrot said that
there's lots of them around.
(then) Oh shit. That's the end
part. I'll start over.

ANGLE - PAST GARY'S HEAD FOCUSING ON REAR VIEW MIRROR

There's a Highway patrol car behind them.

                    GARY (CONT'D)
Shit!!! I've got a cop on my ass!

                    RICK
So ... You didn't do anything
wrong.

                    JEFF
It doesn't matter. They don't
need a reason to pull you over.
Unless, he heard the joke you
just ruined.

                    GARY
               (sarcastically)
Thanks for calming me down Jeff.

                    JEFF
          How fast were you going?

                    GARY
          I don't know. About 85 or 90. I
          was going with traffic.

                    RICK
          You're fucked, man!

The CHP car turns on his lights and siren.

                    GARY
          I told you he's gonna bust me.

                    RICK
          Who told you to go ninety?

                    GARY
          You're a big help... I need to
          know what to say.

                    JEFF
          Offer him a blow job.

                    GARY
          Are you nuts.

                    JEFF
          No ... His nuts. (he laughs)

                    RICK
          Just take the ticket and we'll
          leave.

Gary drives into a turn out. He parks in an area covered by
brush. Rick points to a sign up ahead. It's Zzyzx.

                    RICK
               (excited)
          Guys, it's the Zzyzx sign.

                    GARY
          Why doesn't that make me feel
          better?

The CHP car pulls up to the Honda while maintaining a safe
distance away. His car is also parked in heavy brush.

                    JEFF
          Call you dad. Maybe he knows him.

                    GARY
          Shut the hell up!

The officer exits his car. He puts on his hat and reaches
inside for his ticket book. Then he approaches the boys. The
officer looks inside the car while his hand is on his gun.
Gary holds up his license and he snatches it from him.

                    OFFICER
          You boys are in real trouble.

                    GARY
          All I did was speed.

                    OFFICER
          Looks like two tickets here.

                    JEFF (TO GUYS)
          What an asshole!

The officer walks to the back of the Honda. He indicates the
rear of the car with his nightstick.

                    OFFICER
          What about that busted rear
          light?

                    GARY
          Excuse me officer, but I checked
          this car before we left. All the
          lights were fine.

The Officer walks to the rear of the car and smashes the brake
light. Then, he walks over to his cruiser. He quickly turns
around and yells a command at our boys.

                    OFFICER
          Everyone out of the car and eat
          dirt.

The trio complies. They lie next to each other. The officer returns and begins writing Gary's ticket.

> JEFF
> This guy's nuts.

> GARY
> I shouldn't be getting a ticket.

> OFFICER
> What'd you say punk? I heard that!

> RICK
> Maybe you could give him a warning.

> OFFICER
> (to Jeff)
> And what do you have to say?

> JEFF
> Well, it's not fair that you're driving white cars. You're supposed to be in black and white cars.

> OFFICER
> We change colors to trick "pukes" like you. And see. It works.

Then, WE SEE a bunch of smoke from underneath the Honda. The smoke follows a direct path to the CHP cruiser.

> RICK
> Check out all the smoke.

> JEFF
> I know. It's coming from our car and now it's under his car.

> GARY
> Shouldn't we tell him?

> RICK
> Hell no! Just Shut up.

Our boys begin to cough because of the smoke. Then, a small
fire starts in the brush under the CHP cruiser.

                    RICK
               (to Officer)
          I don't want to tell you your
          business, but shouldn't you do
          something?

                    GARY
          Hey Officer? Your car's on fire.

                    OFFICER
               (not listening)
          Stay on the ground. Mouths shut!

                    JEFF
          Good job man. I see you're in
          control.

Then the officer sees his car on fire and throws his ticket
book and Gary's papers on the hood of Gary's car. Then he
runs over to his car. Flames are everywhere. Then, he uses
his over-the-shoulder radio to summon help.

THE CHP CAR EXPLODES, KNOCKING THE OFFICER TO THE GROUND

                    JEFF
          Let's get the hell out of here.

Everyone gets up. Rick grabs Gary's stuff off the hood along
with the cop's ticket book. Then, they jump in the car and
take off. Gary drives.

                                        CUT TO:

INT. HONDA - CONTINUING

                    GARY
          But he knows who we are.

                    RICK
          He doesn't know us from Adam. And
          right now, he's fucked up!

THEY LAUGH.

                    GARY
          I still think I could have talked
          my way out of the ticket.

                    RICK
          You're nut? He was a real dick!

                                        CUT TO:

HONDA - AS IT PASSED THE ZZYZX SIGN. THE FIRE TRUCKS AND CHP
CARS ARE HEADING IN THE OPPOSITE WAY WITH LIGHTS AND SIRENS.

                    JEFF
          Hey, we just passed the Zzyzx
          sign.

                    RICK
          Shut up Jeff. Nobody gives a shit.

INT. GARY'S CAR - THIRTY MINUTES LATER

There is silence until Gary spots a billboard.

                    GARY
          Hey guys. That sign said the
          world's biggest thermometer is
          ahead.

                    JEFF
          That last sign didn't cause us
          enough trouble.

                    RICK
          Keep driving.

                    GARY
          But, we'll never have another
          chance to see it. The whole world
          knows about it. We've gotta stop.

Rick pulls down his pants.

                    RICK
          Here Gary. The world's biggest
          thermometer. Now, keep driving.

                    GARY
        Yuck!!! Gross man.

                    JEFF
        Do you really want to see it
        Gary?

                    GARY
        Yeah. I really do. Yes.

                    RICK
        What the hell. We deserve a
        reward for blowing up a police
        car.

Rick looks through the stuff he took off the car.

                    RICK (CONT'D)
        Oooh, shit! We've got his ticket
        book.

                    JEFF
        What?
                    RICK
        We got the cop's ticket book and
        all the stuff he wrote down about
        Gary and his car.

                    GARY
        Really? What an idiot. That
        idiot.

                    JEFF
        Hell! Let' s go see a
        thermometer.

                    GARY
        I just saw a sign. We gotta get
        off at the next off ramp.

Gary drives down the off ramp and heads down the road.

                    GARY (CONT ID)
                (excited)
        I can see it from here.

Gary pulls into the entrance. WE SEE a HUGE THERMOMETER.

                    GARY
          I'm gonna park next to that
          building, so this car stays hidden.

                    RICK
          Good idea.

Once again, Gary parks the Honda on top of some brush. No
one notices as they exit the car. They walk away.

This time, it doesn't take long and the brush under the
Honda begins to smoke. No one notices.

                                        CUT TO:

THE BOYS ARE LOOKING AT THE ATTRACTION.

                    JEFF
          Hey Gary. Why are you staring at
          that thing like that?

                    GARY
          I'm waiting for it to change.

Then, a man walks over to Rick with his family. He offers his
camera to Rick.

                    TOURIST
          Excuse me sir, but could you
          please take a picture of my
          family?

                    RICK
          Sure. I'm happy to do it.

Rick takes the camera. He studies it for a second. Then;

                    RICK
          Okay ... Everyone get together
          and smile. (beat) Say cheese.

The whole family begins to cough as some smoke overtakes
them.

                         GROUP
          Just wait for the smoke to go.
          (It passes for a moment)

                         RICK
          Okay, say cheese.

Rick takes the picture. He hands the man back his camera.

                         RICK
          I wonder where that smoke came
          from?

                       LITTLE BOY
                    (points at Honda}
          Over there. That car's on fire.

                         RICK
          What the fuck?

Rick also heads for the Honda, but when he gets there, one
side is completely burned up.

                      RICK (CONT'D)
          Grab whatever you can.

                         GARY
          I'm not touching that thing.

Jeff runs over to the driver's door and opens it. He pulls a
lever and the trunk opens.

                         JEFF
                      (yelling)
          It's spreading.

                         RICK
          Grab anything you can.

Gary runs behind the thermometer as the blaze heads his way.
He pokes his head out.
                         GARY
          Grab my stuff first!

After battling the flames and covering his face with his
shirt, Jeff manages to only save one bag. Everything else in

the trunk goes up in smoke. Rick runs away from the car.

Fire engines show up and douse the car with water along with putting out the fire that spread to the thermometer. Gary approaches the Fire Captain.

> GARY
> What took you guys to long? My car is a charcoal briquette. What am I supposed to do now? Make hot dogs?

> FIRE CAPTAIN
> We would have been here sooner, but would you believe, we just had to put out the same kind of fire up the highway. It's the darndest thing.

The firemen continue to put water on the thermometer and Gary's car as Rick and Jeff approach. Jeff is holding the only piece of luggage that was saved.

> JEFF
> At least I was able to save one bag.

Gary grabs the bag out of Jeff's hand.

> GARY
> It's mine.

> JEFF
> I almost lost my arm in the fire to save your bag.

> GARY
> And look at it now. It's got burn marks all over it.

> RICK
> How about thanking Jeff?

> GARY
> For what? Ruining my bag?

Rick wants to rip Gary's head off.

                    RICK
              (angered)
He risked his life for you. Don't
you have something to say to Jeff.

                    GARY
You' re right ... Jeff, if this
kind of thing ever happens again,
try and grab a matching bag too.

                    JEFF
Rick, I'm gonna kill Gary and no
jury in the world would convict
me!

                    GARY
Look Jeff, if you don't calm down,
I won't get us out of here.

                    JEFF
Oh, I beg your pardon, your
majesty.

Gary walks away and pulls out his cell phone. He makes a
quick call. Then, Gary walks over to Rick and Jeff.

                    GARY
Well, it looks like I saved us.
We'll be out of here in no time.

                    RICK
Okay, but whoever's coming to
pick us up, I' 11 tell them where
to park.

                    GARY
Don't worry. The Desert Sands is
sending a limo for all of us.

                    RICK
Look, I think it's great that a
limo is coming to get us, but in
the meantime, we'd better hide
in case that cop should come over
here.

> JEFF
> I agree. Let's hide behind the
> burned-up thermometer.

The firemen have finished putting out the fire, so our boys
wander over.

> GARY
> Hey Rick. How hot is it?

> RICK
> Gee Gary, I don't know. Why don't
> we look at the destroyed monument
> you burned.

                                        CUT TO:

A distant black limo. It appears to be headed in our
direction.

> JEFF
> There's no way that's for us.

> RICK
> Impossible. It's here too quick.

> GARY
> But, it's coming this way.

The limousine exits the highway and drives up to the boys.

> RICK
> This is crazy!

The boys approach the driver's window. It slides down.

> GARY
> I can't believe you got here so
> fast

> LIMO DRIVER
> I'm sorry gentlemen, but this
> limo spoken for. The current
> owner resides in the back.

Rick opens the back door. We see a small man wearing a small hat. He smokes a cigar which is bigger than he is. His name is Henry.

                    HENRY
          Hi, ya men. What seems to be the
          problem?

                    JEFF
          We need a ride to Vegas. Thank
          God you showed up.

                    HENRY
          I hate to tell you gents, but I'm
                    (HENRY CONT'D)
          not a taxi service. I'm going to
          Vegas, but, I'm flying solo.

                    RICK
          You've got lots of room.

                    HENRY
          And it's all mine... I travel
          alone.

Henry picks up a bottle of booze and pours himself a drink.

                    HENRY (CONT'D)
          How about a drink?

                    RICK
          No, I don't want a drink.

                    HENRY
          Too bad.

Henry reaches across and closes the door. Then, the limo drives off. Our guys are left in a cloud of dust.

                    GARY
          You must have pissed him off.

                    JEFF
          You had to say something to him.

                    RICK
          Not really. He was just a jerk.

The boys head closer to the burned up sign.

> GARY
> We' 11 just wait for the right
> limo, and if I ever see him
> again, I'll kick the shit out of
> him.

Gary reaches into his bag and pulls out a small can. He puts
it under his shirt and moves it around from one side to the
other.

> RICK
> What are you doing?

> GARY
> "Elvis" deodorant. I'm sure we
> could all use some right about
> now.

> RICK
> Are you crazy Gary?

> GARY
> If that guy comes back, I'll beat
> the shit out of him.

> JEFF
> Sure. Now that the guy's gone,
> you've suddenly turned into
> "Rambo"

> GARY
> (changes the subject)
> I can't wait till we get to
> Vegas.

DISSOLVE TO:

THE VEGAS STRIP - TWO HOURS LATER - WE FOLLOW CARS PASSING
ALL THE FANCY HOTELS - WE SEE THE STRANGE PEOPLE AND PLACES
DECORATING THE STRIP - THEN, WE SEE THE DESERT SANDS.

INT. DESERT SANDS HALLWAY - DOORS TO CONFERENCE ROOM

The doors are guarded by one of Joe Vitali' s thugs. Two security guards head down and stop at the first man.

                    FIRST THUG
          Just keep moving.

HE OPENS HIS JACKET EXPOSING A GUN AND HOLSTER. SEEING THIS, THE SECURITY GUARDS CONTINUE BACK THE WAY THEY CAME.

SHOOT THRU TO: INT. CONFERENCE ROOM

There is a big table in the center of the room. Every chair is filled by a member of the mob. They all wear suits. Gary's father sits at the head of the table. He wears gold chains around his neck and gold rings on his fingers. One of the men at the table is named, "Piece". He earned his name for carrying more weapons than anyone else. These men run this hotel. Sal is the first to speak. He is a big man who has eaten much to much pasta over the years.

                      SAL
          I'm ready to talk.

Sal pours a drink and downs it. He quickly pours another.

Little Pauly is next. He too takes a drink. The edges of his suit could gut a fish.

                    PAULY
          I'm ready too. Let's talk ...

Everyone sits.

                    JOE
          I'd like my son Gary to be here,
          but he's not. I sure something
          important is keeping him.

                    SAL
          You know how we all feel about
          Gary. We all love him. He's like
          one of my own. He's like our son
          too.

Joe takes a long drink. Then, he stands.

                    JOE
          Hearing these things warms my
          heart.

"Piece" takes out a gun from his holster and cleans it with
a napkin from the table.

                    JOE (CONT'D)
          And that's why I'm gonna say what
          I have to say. (beat) My father
          and grandfather started this thing
          of ours. We're all family. But
          my son, Gary, well ... somehow,
          he doesn't belong. And there's
          only one way to say it. (beat) He
          will never be one of us. Like they
          say, ... either you've got it or
          you ain't and Gary ain't got it.
          No one should think less of him.
          He could never be an earner but,
          he'll always be my son. So, I want
          it clear with all the families
          that my son is and will always be
          a citizen ... That's it!!!

Everyone in the room ad- libs agreement with Joe. They stand
up and, one at a time embrace Joe and pat him on his back.
Everyone takes their seat.

                    JOE
          Now, we have some pressing
          business

                                        CUT TO:

EXT - NIGHT - HOURS LATER

The limo carrying Gary, Rick and Jeff enters the driveway to
the Desert Sands.

                                        CUT TO:

INT. LIMO - CONTINUING

The boys have been drinking from the limo's bar. The limo
stops at the hotel entrance and a valet opens the door.

                         VALET
          Welcome to the Desert Sands.

All three boys try and exit at the same time.

                         RICK
               (to Jeff)
          If you knew how to drive we'd be
          in a Honda Accord

                         JEFF
          I wasn't driving - "dip shit"
          It's Gary's fault. He drove his
          car.

                         RICK
               (remembering)
          Oh yeah ... Him and his stupid
          jokes.

                         JEFF
               (to Gary)
          Gary, Take care of the limo guy.

                         GARY
          The Hotel takes care of it.

                         RICK
          No they don't. Just tip the guy.

                         GARY
          Okay.

Gary hands the limo driver a few chips. Gary walks away. The
limo driver looks at the chips and chases after Gary.

                         VALET
          Excuse me sir. These are poker
          chips from your home.

Gary takes back the chips and Rick gives the Valet real
money.

                         VALET
          Thank you, sir.

                    RICK
I'm sorry. My friend's an idiot.

                    GARY
I'll pay you back. I'm not an
idiot

                    JEFF
You mean, you dad's gonna pay me.

                    GARY
Shut the hell up! You guys are
a bunch of assholes. And for
your information, my dad's a
businessman.

                    RICK
So was Al Capone.

                    JEFF
C'mon. We're here to have fun and
not call Gary's dad a gangster.

                    GARY
Fuck both of you!

                    JEFF
Just answer me one more question.

                    GARY
What?

                    JEFF
How many license plates can your
dad make in an hour?

                    GARY
Fuck you Jeff! Get your own room.

                    RICK
C'mon Gary. He was just screwing
around. Let's have fun, all
right?

                    GARY
I don't appreciate all those

(GARY CONT'D)
jokes about my dad. So knock it
off.

Jeff looks around. He's very excited.

                    JEFF
        We sure went through a lot to get
        here.

                    GARY
        I love it here. I love Vegas.

                    RICK
        Greatest place in the world.

Gary picks up his bag that someone put by him.

                    JEFF
        One lousy bag. And it's Gary's.

                    GARY
        God must have wanted my bag to
        live

                    JEFF
        It's your fault Gary. I checked
        looked under your car. For some
        reason, that car didn't have a
        heat shield under it. It caused
        both fires to happen.

                    GARY
        We didn't get caught, did we?

                    RICK
        No, but you did. You're buying us
        all new clothes.

Gary sees a Valet walking by. Gary stops him.

                    GARY
        Excuse me sir, but do you know a
        valet named, Gig?

                    2ND VALET

Of course I do. Mr. Gig is in
charge of all valets.

                    GARY
Thanks.

                    2ND VALET
Shall I tell him who's calling.

                    GARY
Gary Vitali.

                    2ND VALET
               (taken aback)
Are you related to Mr. Joe
Vitali?

                    GARY
He' s my father.

                    2ND VALET
I see. Are you gentlemen checked
in?

                    GARY
No. We just got here.

                    2ND VALET
I'll take care of everything.

The Valet hurries away.

                    GARY
What do you think of my dad now?

                    RICK
I think he's a crook and a
killer.

                    GARY
Asshole! Just for that, you have
to tip the valet. I already did.

                    RICK
          I give him real money and not
          fake chips from your house.

The limo driver approaches Gary.

                    VALET
          Will there be anything else
          gentlemen?

                    RICK
          C'mon Gary. Give him something
          else

                    GARY
               (pissed)
          You're all trying to screw me!

Gary pulls out his wallet and looks inside. He closes it.

                    GARY (CONT'D)
          I'm a little short.

                    JEFF
          How about the money in your
          wallet? It's behind a picture of
          yourself.

                    GARY
          My wallet's private. How'd you
          know about that?

                    RICK
          Just pay him.

Gary again takes out his wallet and pulls out money which he
gives to the limo driver.

                    DRIVER
          Thank you sir.

The driver heads back towards his limo.

                    GARY
          You guys happy now?

                    JEFF
          Not really. I'm afraid you've got
          another joke to tell.

                    RICK
          Hey you guys. Now we have to take
          taxis all over town.

                    GARY
          You're are blaming me for
          everything, aren't you?

                    RICK
          Well, let's see. There's now two
          good cars less in the world.
          Whose fault do you suppose that
          is?

                    GARY
          My new friend is the Valet. Not
          you.

                    JEFF
            That's because he's afraid of you.

The Valet returns and hands everyone a key-card.

                    VALET
          These are your room cards.

                    JEFF
          Is this a noisy floor?

                    VALET
          No sir. The floor is yours alone.

The guys kind of <u>giggle</u> to each other.

                                        CUT TO:

INT. ELEVATOR - THE DOOR CLOSES

                    VALET
          In order to get to your floor or
          room, you'11 need to slide the
          key into this slot. It'll take

(VALET CONT'D)
you right to your penthouse or
floor.

The Valet indicates that all the floor lights are lit.

VALET (CONT'D)
I don't know how it happened, but
all the floor buttons are lit up.

RICK
You mean we're gonna stop on each
damn floor?

Then, from behind the Valet, out steps a little man. IT'S
HENRY! CIGAR AND ALL.

As the men talk, the elevator door opens and closes on each
floor.

HENRY
Hi men. Ah, sorry about my
little prank, but when I hit the
buttons, no one else was in the
elevator. You guys came in at the
last second.

RICK
That's great! We're stuck with
him!

GARY
Aren't you the guy in the limo
who wouldn't give us a ride to
Vegas?

Jeff realizes that for once, Gary is right.

JEFF
I should slam your head into the
card slot you little shit!

HENRY
I'm truly sorry men.

                    VALET
And what floor will you be
departing.

                    HENRY
Two.

                    JEFF
This is your idea of fun. There's
a whole casino full of games and
you come in here. What a dumb
jerk!

                    HENRY
That's me.

INT. TOP FLOOR PENTHOUSE - THE ELEVATOR DOOR OPENS ALL-EXIT

The Valet uses the card and opens the door to the penthouse.

The Valet grabs Henry by the collar and pulls him back into
the elevator. Rick and Jeff pull out some money and hand it
to the Valet.

                    VALET
By the way gentlemen, this entire
floor belongs to you.

The Valet waves off Rick and Jeff. He won't take money

                    VALET (CONT'D)
No thank you men. You have been
more than entertaining.

The Valet rushes in when he sees Henry pushing buttons.

                    VALET (CONT'D)
Oh, no you don't.

The elevator door closes.

                    RICK
Hey Gary, I didn't see you
offering the Valet any money.

Jeff closes the door to their penthouse.

                    GARY
          I was going to. I was giving him
          a hundred.

                    JEFF
          I didn't see that. You must be a
          better magician than Houdini.

The guys walk around the penthouse.

                    RICK
          This is some room.

                    JEFF
          No shit! Hey, you think Gary's
          dad knows he's here?

                    RICK
          From the size of this room, I
          think he's got a pretty good
          idea.

                    GARY
          Now maybe you guys will start
          glving me the respect I deserve

Rick starts removing his clothes down to his shorts.

                    RICK
          Gary, nothing' s changed. You're
          still you and if you want
          respect, you'll give respect.

Rick jumps into the hot tub.

                    JEFF
          That looks like a good idea.

Jeff strips down and joins Rick.

                    RICK
          Don't be a chicken, Gary. Jump
          in. At least you have fresh
          clothes.

SFX - KNOCKING AT THE DOOR

Gary answers the door and is handed an envelope by a Valet.
He looks at the message inside. Gary closes the door on him.

                    JEFF
          What's the message? Is it for us?

                    GARY
          I gotta go.

                    RICK
          Did daddy send for you?

                    GARY
          Screw you Rick. I gotta go.

Gary opens the door and is surprised by three girls who walk
right past him. Rick yells out.

                    RICK
          Don't leave now. One's for you.

                                        DISSOLVE TO:

INT. HOTEL CONFERENCE ROOM - MINUTES LATER

The door opens and Gary sheepishly walks in.

                    JOE
          My son, everyone.

Joe pulls on a chair next to his, but Pauly is in it.

                    JOE (CONT'D)
          Hey Pauly. You need an
          invitation?

Pauly gets up and takes another seat. Gary walks over to his
father. They hug and pat each other on the back.

                    GARY
          It's good to see you dad.

                    JOE
          Sit down next to me, my son.

Gary takes his seat. All the men "ad-lib" their greetings.

                    JOE (CONT'D)
I'm glad my son is with me to
share the last days of The Desert
Sands.

                    GARY
I'm glad I'm here too, dad. I
hate to see it close.

                    SAL
Hey kid. How's about you doin'
that Elvis thing you do?

                    JOE
Fellas ... fellas. I didn't ask
my son to come into this room to
put on an act. What I have to
say is serious. Now Gary. I'd
like you to come back here in two
hours. (beat) Now leave us.

                                        GARY EXITS:

                                        DISSOLVE TO:

INT. CASINO - ONE HOUR LATER - NIGHT

Gary walks through the casino and stops at a blackjack
table. He sees an open spot and puts a hundred-dollar bill
on it. The cards are dealt face up and Gary get's blackjack.
Then, the dealer exposes her hand and she too has twenty-
one. She collects everyone's money, but when she comes to
Gary's hand, she lightly hits the table. It's a "push." Gary
takes his money off the table.

                    GARY
                 (to himself)
I can't even win with a
blackjack.

A man moves in front of Gary and sits down. It's Henry.

                    HENRY
Hi ya pal. I just saw what
happened ... Tough break.

                         GARY
          I'll break you in two, you worm!

                                             CUT TO:

PENTHOUSE - CONTINUING

Jeff and Rick are in the hot tub with girls. They are all
naked and are jumping all over each other having fun.

                                             CUT TO:

CASINO BAR - MINUTES LATER

Gary gets up with a drink in hand and walks through the
casino. As he does, several men in suits say "hello" to him.
To them, he is Mr. Vitali. A man to be respected.

                         STRANGERS
          Hello Mr. Vitali - Hello sir -
          ...

Gary makes it to the elevator as it's door opens. He steps
inside and the door closes.

                                             QUICK CUT:

ELEVATOR BOARD - ALL BUTTONS ARE LIT UP

Seeing this, Gary downs his drink. Then, he spots Henry.

                         GARY
               Oh shit! You did the buttons
               again. You little asshole!!!

                         HENRY
               Sorry about that. I didn't know
               it was you. There's a lot of
               elevators.

                         GARY
               And you stole my black jack
               chair.

                         HENRY
               Yeah! Who would believe it? I

won four hands in a row. Two were
black jacks. I was really lucky.

> GARY
> I don't want to hear that. At
> least tell me you lost your ass!

> HENRY
> Okay. I lost.

> GARY
> No you didn't.

> HENRY
> I know. Isn't it great?

> GARY
> And stop it with the buttons.

The elevator continues to stop at each floor. The doors open
and close.

> HENRY
> How about if I split what I won
> at the table with you?

> GARY
> How much did you win?
> HENRY
> Ten dollars. Wasn't I lucky?

> GARY
> You can't even kill a guy for
> that!

Henry reaches into his pocket and pulls out a few dollars.

> GARY (CONT'D)
> (incredulously)
> Ten dollars? You won four hands
> with two black jacks and all you
> won is ten dollars. (a beat) Do
> you have any idea how much I
> would have won with that winning
> streak? My first hand alone would
> have been a hundred. And take

                    (GARY CONT'D)
          another elevator. There's six
          more elevators that don't go to
          the penthouse.

                    HENRY
          I don't know what to say.

                    GARY
          You need a doctor. A shrink.

                    HENRY
          You' re right. You're exactly
          right. It's a sickness. (beat)
          Why didn't I see this before.

THE ELEVATOR KEEPS STOPPING AT EVERY FLOOR. THE DOOR OPENS
AND THEN CLOSES.

                    GARY
          You don't have any idea who I am?
          If I wanted to, I could squash
          you like a bug. With one word,
          you'd be toast. One word. I'm not
          kidding.

                    HENRY
          I get it. You're a scary guy.

The elevator door opens and Henry exits.

Then, he realizes that he's on the wrong floor and quickly
darts back inside.

                    GARY
          See how you screw everything up.
          You can't even pick your own
          floor.

                    HENRY
          You're right. I've got nine more
          to go. I pretend that I'm at
          a ball game and the floors are
          innings. Like now. It's the first
          inning.

The door to the second floor opens.

> GARY
>
> What do you know. Game called
> because of an idiot. It's the
> second floor. Get the hell out!

Henry heads out and turns back for one more thing.

> HENRY
>
> You don't have to be so mean.

> GARY
>
> I just want you out of my life. I
> have my own friends.

The elevator door closes as Henry stares in at Gary.

                                        CUT TO:

INT. PENTHOUSE - CONTINUING

Rick and Jeff are having a blast. While one girl is naked in
the hot tub with Rick, Jeff chases the other two naked girls
back into the bedroom.

PENTHOUSE - DOORBELL RINGS - (SFX) - GARY OPENS THE DOOR AND
GREETS HIS ASIAN HOOKER. (SHE'S EASY TO SPOT. HER DRESS IS
UP TO HER ASS AND SHE HAS A TINY PURSE WHICH JUST HAS ENOUGH
ROOM FOR SMOKES, A CONDOM AND MONEY.

                                        CUT TO:

INT. HOTEL ROOM - MINUTES LATER

> GARY
>
> Since I'm paying for this ...
> call me Elvis.

> PROSTITUTE
>
> Are you nuts or something?

> GARY
>
> Well, that's what I want ...
> (Pause) No tickie--No laundry. No

                    (GARY CONT'D)
money.

                    PROSTITUTE
That make no sense. You make no
sense. You watch too much T.V.
for a white boy.

                GARY (Perplexed)
If that's dirty talk, it's not
getting me hard.

                    PROSTITUTE
If you want romance, ... it gonna
cost you fifty more. That's the
tickie you get with laundry, fat
boy Elvis. You get it?

Gary grabs her hand and leads her into his room.

                        GARY
Fuck it! Let's do it. (To
everyone) I think I love her.

                                        CUT TO:

INT. GARY'S ROOM

He can't shed his clothes fast enough, but the hooker is
still dressed.

                        GARY
Let's fuck already.

The Hooker takes Gary's hand and leads him into the
bathroom.

                        HOOKER
You come with me first.

Gary protests as she squats down. Gary doesn't like this one
bit.

                        GARY
What the hell are you doing? Is
this some kind of kinky foreplay?

The Hooker examines Gary's genitals and surrounding area as if she were a doctor.

                    GARY (CONT'D)
          So, blow me already.

                    HOOKER
          You look okay to me. Let's go to
          bed now.

She gets up and goes over to the bed with Gary in tow.

                    GARY
          What the hell were you doing???
          Checking me out???

                    HOOKER
          You clean like little fat boy.

                    GARY
          I said, call me Elvis and while
          we're on the Subject, ... (PAUSE}
          Who the hell examines you???

                    PROSTITUTE
          You don't have to worry about me.
          I clean as a whistle.

She beckons Gary to join her.

                    GARY
          I've seen a lot of crappy
          whistles in my day.

                    PROSTITUTE
          Come over here. I'm ready to suck
          Elvis dick now.

Gary finally joins her in bed.

                    GARY
          It's about time you realize that
          I'm your master.

                                        CUT TO:

INT. PENTHOUSE MAIN ROOM - THIRTY MINUTES LATER

TIGHT SHOT ON ELEVATOR DOOR - IT OPENS AND GARY EXITS

The elevator door closes behind Gary and he enters the penthouse. Rick's in the tub with one of the girls.

> RICK
>
> C'mon Gary. Take your clothes off
> and come in.

> FIRST GIRL
> (playfully)
> Yeah. Get naked with us. Let's
> fuck

Gary's mood changes.

> GARY
> Do I get to pick the girl I want?

ANGLE ON BEDROOM - JEFF EXITS

Jeff has his arm around each girl. They're all drunk.

> JEFF
>
> What's going on?

> RICK
> Gary wants one for himself.

> JEFF
> (it's a real orgy!)
> Ought of sight.

> RICK
> If my friend wants his own girl,
> then he gets his own girl. And
> by the way Jeff, I haven't heard
> anyone say, "out of sight" since
> I saw a "Monkees" movie.

> GARY
>
> I liked it.

                    RICK
          Never mind that. Take her Gary.

Gary points at Rick's girl.

                    GARY
          I want her. At least I know she's
          clean since she's been in that
          hot tub.

Rick pushes a girl out of the tub. Gary motions to her.

                    GARY (CONT'D)
          C'mon honey. Let's hit the
          bedroom.

She wraps a towel around her and walks past Gary and into
the bedroom.

                    GARY
          This is like a dream.

                    GIRLS VOICE FROM BEDROOM
          C'mon baby. Let's get wild.

                    GARY
          I'll just be a minute.

Gary is visibly nervous.
                    RICK
          Get your ass in there!

Gary heads into the bedroom. He slams the door shut.

INT. PENTHOUSE - FIFTEEN MINUTES LATER

Gary exits the bedroom wearing his underpants. They have
little pictures of "Elvis" on them. He's very excited.

                    GARY
               (whispering)
          Guys ... I need a favor. Fast!

                    RICK AND JEFF
          What?

GARY

She said that if I got another
girl, I could screw both of them
at the same time. A threesome!
Do you believe it? Me, in a
threesome.

RICK

Just a minute. I'm just trying to
wrap my brain around that one.

JEFF

Ditto.

RICK

You could have one of these
babes, but, they're straight.
Strictly guys.

JEFF

Maybe he means one at a time?

GARY

Cause, there are a lot of
prophylactic chicks in those
countries and she'll only
do it with a chick who's a
prophylactic.

RICK

You idiot!!! She's talking about
a rubber. You need a rubber or
she won't screw you.

GARY

Screw you Rick! I've screwed more
chicks than you. At least a hundred.

JEFF

This isn't a contest.

GARY

So, do I get a rubber or not?

RICK

Sure. (beat) There's one in. the

                         (RICK CONT'D)
          ash tray next to the bed. Just
          wash it out and use the damn
          thing.

Gary starts for the bedroom. Then,

                         GARY
          I better not be getting "sloppy
          seconds", Rick.

                                        GARY EXITS:

                         RICK
          I'd never give you "sloppy"
          seconds ... Maybe "sloppy"
          thirds.

                         GARY (V.O.)
          Here I am baby. I just need to
          find an ash tray. (THEN) No! No!
          Don't put your cigarette out in
          that.

                                        DISSOLVE TO:

INT. PENTHOUSE - ANGLE ON BEDROOM

Gary exits in a panicked state. He's visibly shaken.

                         GARY
          Everyone's gotta go!

Jeff's in the hot tub with two girls.

                         JEFF
          Are you kiddin' I'm staying like
          this until I lose my hard on.

Gary goes around the room picking up clothes and throwing
them at the girls. He's tossing girls clothes at guys etc
...

                         GARY
          All you girls have to split.
          Now!!!

The girls exit the hot tub and sort through the clothes. The other girl joins in.

> RICK
> Gary, what's going on? You're
> acting like a mad man.

> GARY
> Just get the fuck dressed. We
> gotta leave. They know where we
> are.

> JEFF
> Who? Who knows where we are?

> RICK
> Half the people here know where
> to find us.

The girls head for the door. He points to money on the bar.

> GARY
> Your monies on the bar.

The girls collect their money and exit through the door.

> RICK
> Look Gary. We're not moving one
> inch until you tell us what's
> going on. You know, we have a
> right to know too.

> GARY
> Okay, here it is. If we stay
> in here, we'll probably get
> murdered.

> RICK
> If that's the case, (he panics)
> Let's get the hell out!

> GARY
> Yeah. It's me and anyone who's with
> me.

                    JEFF
          C'mon Rick. Why don't we go to
          the casino and call Gary in an
          hour. We'll just check in with
          him.

                    GARY
          I'm glad I have such loyal
          friends.

                    RICK
          He's only kidding.

                    JEFF
          I was?

                    RICK
          Look, Gary. What can we do to
          help?

                    GARY
          We gotta leave this place as fast
          as humanly possible.

                    JEFF
          Does this have anything to do
          with your father?

                    RICK
          Shut up Jeff. Just get dressed.

Rick and Jeff throw their clothes on and wait by the door.

EXT. DOOR IN HALLWAY BEFORE ELEVATOR

Then, Gary comes bolting out of his bedroom and past the
open door. They press the button for the elevator.

                    JEFF
            This better not be bull shit,
            Gary.

TIGHT SHOT ON ELEVATOR DOOR - IT OPENS

Henry is clearly visible. Rick spots him first. He grabs him.

> RICK
> I can't deal with this guy now!

> HENRY
> (sheepishly)
> Hi ya men. How's about giving me
> a quick tour of your place?

> JEFF
> You want a tour?

Jeff grabs Henry away from Rick and flings him across the
room. Henry falls over the couch and lands in the hot tub.

> JEFF (CONT'D)
> That's the tour. How'd you like
> it?

Everyone enters the elevator and it closes.

HENRY SPITS WATER OUT OF HIS MOUTH AS HE SITS IN THE HOT TUB

INT. ELEVATOR - CONTINUING

> JEFF
> We were having a great time.

> GARY
> I just probably saved your lives.
> You could have been mowed down
> like sitting ducks. Believe me.

> RICK
> What's happening to our vacation?

> CUT TO:

EXT. HOTEL CONFERENCE HALL -

Gary enters the conference room. A guard stops him.

> GARY
> My dad sent for me.

Gary stands in a corner and watches a man with his hands in

a cupped position. Joe puts a religious card in the man's hands and lights it on fire. Joe doesn't know that Gary's watching, or does he?

                    JOE (LOUDLY)
          As this card burns in your
          hands, so may your soul burn in
          everlasting hell, if you should
          ever betray this family or
          organization.

The card burns out and Vic, one of Joe's men, wipes his hands together. Sal hands him a towel. Then, the men in the room clap.

Suddenly, from behind, Gary is pushed into the room. He approaches his father as the men in the room congratulate the new member.

In the b.g. everyone makes toasts to the new man in their family. Joe chooses to concentrate on Gary.

                    JOE
          You're late! I happen to know
          what was going on with those
          hookers and your friends.

                    GARY
          I'm sorry dad.

                    JOE
          For what? You did use a rubber,
          didn't you?

                    GARY
          Of course.

                    JOE
          Never apologize for getting laid.
          (He laughs)

Joe changes his tune. He makes an announcement to everyone.

                    JOE
               (yelling)
          All right ... Everyone out! Get

                    (JOE CONT'D)
          the fuck out now!

Gary heads for the door. Joe sees this and shakes his head.

                         JOE
                    (yelling)
          Not you Gary! Come here.

Everyone in the room has left. Gary and Joe are the only
one's left. Gary is nervous.

                         GARY
          Thanks for the great room dad.

                         JOE
          I hope you and your friends
          are having a great time. Just
          consider this place your castle
          and you guys are the kings.

                         GARY
          It's a great place. We love it.

                         JOE
          Good. Now sit down so we can
          talk. (beat) What I have to say
          is serious. (beat) you know, a
          minute ago, you were looking in
          on a sacred ceremony.

                         GARY
          I know. It looked serious.

                         JOE
          You were spying! I hate spies!

                         GARY
          I was just curious.

                         JOE
                    (his tone changes)
          Don't interrupt! Don't ever
          interrupt me! (beat) Now, I've
          always taken care of you and you
          know that one day, when your time

came, I would take you into the
family business. (beat) You know
what I do and who I am. (beat)
You've always known.

> GARY

You're my dad. You run a big
company with a lot of guys around
you.

> JOE
>> (laughs)

Thanks for the snow job, but
neither of us believes that
bull ... Do we?

> GARY

Not really. I know what goes on.
I try and keep my eyes closed,
but I see pretty well.

> JOE

Then, you also know that one day it
would be time for you to step up,
so to speak and join the business.
Father and son. Like I've always
dreamed.

> GARY
>> (incredulously)

You mean, I'm gonna be a <u>made</u>
guy?

> JOE

No.

> GARY

No?

> JOE

Nope.

Joe takes Gary's arm and leads him to the couch.

                        JOE
          Here. Sit.

Gary sits in the corner of the couch. He's confused

                        GARY
          Did I screw up? Was it the police
          car I blew up? Or was it my Honda
          and the thermometer I destroyed?

                        JOE
          What are you talking about?

                        GARY
                (Gary changes course)
          Nothing. Just kid's stuff.

                        JOE
          Gary. You're my son. My flesh and
          blood. But, about making you a
          part of what I do, well ... I
          just don't think it's the right
          move. This thing of ours is just
          not what you're looking for.
          It's just not in your blood and
          I can't do it. But, there's just
          one problem? (beat) Someone wants
          you dead.

                        GARY
          Someone wants me dead?

                        GARY
          You don't mean, "dead!" Like dead
          dead! Do you? I thought all the
          guys love me.

                        JOE
          I guess all, but one. But, don't
          worry. I've got everyone looking
          after you.

Joe goes over to the bar. He opens a drawer and pulls out a
gun. He walks over to Gary and hands him the gun and a box.

                    GARY
    I'm no good with guns.

                    JOE
    That's what killer's count on.

                    GARY
    Killers!

Gary accidentally drops the gun on the floor. He quickly
picks it up. He hopes that his father didn't see that. Joe
goes back into the drawer and brings out a shoulder holster.
He forces Gary to take it.

                    JOE
        Get used to wearing this. And get
        used to pulling it out and firing.
        (beat) Hopefully, you won't miss.

                    GARY
    What about my friends?

                    JOE
        If you accidently kill one of
        them, just call me. (beat) I'll
        have some of the boys pick up the
        body. It'll be as if they were
        never here.

                    GARY
        But I like my friends. What do I
        tell them?

                    JOE
            (impatiently)
        Nothing! Tell them nothing. Lie.

                    GARY
    Why don't I just fly home?

                    JOE
        No! I need to find out who isn't
        loyal to our family. Stay with
        your friends and groups of
        people. It'll be harder to kill
        you. But for now, don't trust

                    (JOE CONT'D)
          anyone, but try and have a good
          time. Remember. You're my son. (a
          beat) Be tough!

                    GARY
          How can I have a good time when
          someone's trying to kill me?

                    JOE
          I live with fear every day. It
          comes with being the boss.

                                    DISSOLVE TO:

INT. CASINO - ONE HOUR LATER - NIGHT

Gary walks through the casino. He stops at a blackjack
table. He sees a card on the table informing the players
that it is a one-hundred-dollar table. Gary reaches into his
pocket and pulls out a hand full of black chips. He takes a
seat.
Next to Gary sits a very attractive woman. They're about the
same age. She puts her hand on Gary's arm.

                         WOMAN
               You don't want to waste your
               money. This dealer's been killing
               us.

                         GARY
               Are you still playing?

She waves her hand over her spot indicating that she's out.

                         GARY
               Maybe I can change the luck here.

Gary pulls five black chips and throws them down.

                    GARY (CONT'D)
                    (confident)
               Let's go!

The dealer deals out all the hands. Gary gets blackjack

                    WOMAN
               (aghast)
          Oh my god! You've got twenty-one!

                    GARY
          I know. I know.

Gary leaves his money out and stacks the chips together. The
dealer deals out the cards. Gary gets twenty.

                    GARY
               (to woman)
          What's your name?
                    JANE
          Jane.

Gary wins the hand and pulls back his money. He gives Jane a
black chip.

                    JANE (CONT'D)
          What's this for?

                    GARY
          For luck. I wouldn't have won the
          hand without you.

                    JANE
               (rubs his arm)
          You're so nice.

Gary is very pleased. He gets up from the table.

                    JANE (CONT'D)
          Where to honey?

                    GARY
          Sorry. I gotta go.

                    JANE
          Can't we go there together?

                    GARY
          No offense, but I got business.
          Maybe I'll see you later.

Gary turns and disappears into the crowd. Jane's not happy.

                                              CUT TO:

GARY ENTERS THE ELEVATOR AND QUICKLY EXITS

Henry follows him out.

                    GARY
          I could kill you. Can't you use
          another elevator?

                    HENRY
          It's the only glass elevator.

                    GARY
          How about if I pry the elevator
          door open and I shove you down
          the shaft?

                    HENRY
          I'm sorry. I'm sorry.

Henry keeps repeating that as he walks away towards the
casino. Gary waits for the next elevator.

                                              CUT TO:

INT. PENTHOUSE - MINUTES LATER

Gary walks in as three girls rush past him and out the door.

                    GARY
          What's going on? Why are they
          back?

Jeff and Rick are both wearing hotel bathrobes. They plop
down on the nearest chair. Glasses full of booze are all
around.

                    GARY (CONT'D)
          You were supposed to meet me in
          the casino.

                    RICK
          Don't talk to me. Talk to "Long
          Dong Silver" over there.

                    JEFF
          Look man. Shit just happens.
          What do you think? I did it on
          purpose?

                    RICK
              You're a "perv"!

                    GARY
          What the hell are you talking
          about?

                    JEFF
          Didn't you ever "cross swords?"

                    RICK
          Don't even say that! It's sick!
          (to Jeff) You're sick!

                    JEFF
          It couldn't be helped. It was
          funny. Even the chicks laughed.

                    RICK
          That's cause they're chicks. They
          don't have "schlongs"!

Rick gets up and slides on a pair of shorts. He takes off his
robe.

                    GARY
          Where'd you get the shorts?

                    RICK
          We bought a bunch of stuff and
          charged it to the room.

Rick heads for the door and opens it.

                    RICK (CONT'D)
          I'm going to the pool. (to Jeff)
          And get over this "crossing
          swords" shit My sword was crossed
          over too. Get over it already.

                    GARY
So, big deal. It's happened to
me.

                    JEFF
Now I know you're lying. You've
never had a threesome.

                    GARY
Fuck you Jeff.

                    RICK
So our dicks crossed. So what?

                    JEFF
Ha, ha. Our dicks crossed. Now,
we're "X-Men!"

                    GARY
I love watching you guys fighting,
when it's not about me. It's
funny.

                    JEFF
What do you think is so funny?

                    RICK
This whole thing is crazy.

                    JEFF
Just don't ever mention it again.

Jeff walks over to the dresser and opens it, then quickly
shuts it.

                    RICK
What's wrong?

                    JEFF
There's a gun and bullets in
there.

Gary walks over to the drawer and opens it. He picks up the
gun and puts it into his holster. Then he gathers up the
bullets and loads them into a couple of clips.

                    RICK
You met with your father didn't
you.

                    GARY
Yeah. So what? It's my business.

                    RICK
So it is true. Your dad brought
you up here to bring you into his
den of thieves and turn you into
some kind of "goodfella!"

                    GARY
You've seen too many movies.

                    JEFF
All right. Then tell us what's
going on? And remember. If you
lie, we can tell.

Gary puts the clip in the gun and puts it away.

                    GARY
My dad turned me down. I'm not a
"goodfella," ... a mob guy ...
or a made guy. I'm just dumbass
Gary. I got kicked out before I
got in.

                    RICK
I don't get. If you're not
involved, then why the gun and
stuff?

                    GARY
Cause, someone really is out
there to kill me. They don't like
the idea that I'm not with the
family.

                    JEFF
This means that we're all
targets?

                    GARY
          That's right.

                    RICK
          You know, if you do the right
          thing, you'll be protecting Jeff
          and me. And we'll never forget
          you.

                    GARY
          Fuck you. I'm not gonna kill
          myself.

                  RICK AND JEFF
                    (laughing)

                    RICK
          So will you now admit that your
          dad is in the Mafia?

                    GARY
          All right. Fine. My dad's in the
          Mafia. He's in the mob. He's a
          crook. He's a goodfella. (beat)
          Are you happy now?

                    JEFF
          You're a real blabbermouth. Your
          business is your business.

                    GARY
          You're both assholes!

Jeff slides on a pair of shorts and loses the bathrobe. He
heads for the door.

                    JEFF
          Well, let's not let this spoil
          our vacation. Let's hit the pool.

                    GARY
          And what am I supposed to do?

                    RICK
          You're right.

Rick goes over to the phone and picks it up.

                    GARY
               (to Jeff)
          You'd better not say one word
          about what you know.

                    JEFF
          Who am I gonna tell? Don
          Corleone?

Gary sees Rick on the phone

                    GARY
          Who you calling Rick?

                    RICK
          The F.B.I. or the police. We
          need protection. We need witness
          protection. I want another
          identity.

Gary grabs the phone and slams it down.

                    GARY
          Are you nuts? Just chill.

                    JEFF
          I'd feel a lot better if the cops
          were chilling with me.

                    RICK
          If you're the target, why do Jeff
          and I have to worry?

                    GARY
          Cause, they'll use you guys to
          get to me. That's why.

Rick pulls a knife out of his pocket and approaches Gary.
Then, (to Jeff)

                    RICK
          Bring me the joker card from
          that deck of cards that's on the

table.

Jeff goes over to the table and goes through the cards. He pulls out a joker and gives it to Rick. Then, Rick goes over to Gary.

               RICK
    We'll be comfortable over here.

Rick pulls Gary over to the table.

               RICK (CONT'D)
    Sit down.

               GARY
    What the hell are you doing?

Rick produces his knife.

               RICK
    This is the answer to your
    problem. I know how to fix this.
    See, I give you a little prick
    with the knife and we burn the
    card. Then you're a "made man."
    Then, you'll be one of them.
               GARY
       (getting up)
    You're fuckin' nuts!

               RICK
    Can't say I didn't try.

Rick heads for the door.

               RICK (CONT'D)
    C'mon Jeff. Let's go downstairs.

               GARY
    You guys are supposed to be my
    friends. All you want to do
    is leave me alone. What am I
    supposed to do?

               RICK
    Pretend you get in trouble, we'll

be right behind you.

                    JEFF
About two miles behind.

                    RICK
I'm serious Jeff. Gary didn't know
that this shit was gonna go down.
We came here for a vacation.

                    GARY
Thanks guys. You're good friends.

                    JEFF
          (to Gary)
You know that new I-phone you
got?

                    GARY
What about it?

                    JEFF
Can I have first dibs on it if
anything happens to you?
                    GARY
No! That's brand new.

                    RICK
C'mon Jeff. Let's do this shit
as a team. As a matter of fact.
Let's all change and hit the
casino.

                    JEFF
Good idea.

                    GARY
And I know just what to wear.

Gary goes over to the mini bar and sees that it's empty.

                    GARY (CONT'D)
          (pissed)
What the fuck happened here?

                    RICK

Those chicks really packed it in.

              GARY
Thanks a lot. Was it worth it?

              JEFF
You'd better believe it. Now
I know why they call it a
butterfinger.

              GARY
You're an asshole Jeff.

              RICK
Just get dressed okay?

Everyone retires into their bedrooms.

                                      CUT TO:

ACTION IN THE CASINO AT VARIOUS TABLE GAMES AND SLOT
MACHINES
- THERE'S A LINE FOR THE BUFFET AND FOR THE SHOW

                                      CUT TO:
INT. PENTHOSE - THIRTY MINUTES LATER

              RICK (V.O.)
You guys ready to leave yet?

Jeff enters the main room. He's dressed in slacks and a nice
sport's jacket. Unfortunately, since Gary picked it out, it
doesn't fit quite right. And when Rick comes out, he has the
same problem with his clothes.

              JEFF
I think we could use a tailor?

WE NOTICE a table full of food in the center of the room

              GARY (V.O.)
Did room service come yet.

Jeff and Rick are stuffing their faces.

                    RICK
          No not yet.

Gary enters the room. He's still wearing the same clothes.

                    GARY
          I just talked to my dad.

                    RICK
          And ...
                    GARY
               (disappointed)
          He can't do anything. He's trying
          to find the guy, but he can't.

                    JEFF
          That sucks.

                    GARY
          What should our next move be?

                    JEFF
          Well, they can't stop our fun.

Gary joins in and has some shrimp from one of the trays. Jeff
and Rick are pretty full. The boys head for the door.

                    RICK
          There's three of us and one of
          him.

                    JEFF
          We got this thing covered. Maybe,
          he'll just change his mind.

                    GARY
          I'm glad you guys are so at ease.

                                        CUT TO:

INT. CASINO AREA - MINUTES LATER

Our guys walk through the casino and look around. Gary looks
back and forth like a chicken.

                         GARY
             Remember. You guys just keep moving
             around me and It'll be safer.

                         JEFF
                  (to Rick) (whispering)
             I hope this guy's a good shot. He
             could accidentally shoot me!

Gary takes a small box out of his pocket and hands it to
Jeff. He opens it. It's a beautiful watch.

                         JEFF
                  (putting on watch)
             I don't know how to thank you.

                         GARY
             You'll know when the time comes.

                         RICK
                  (jealous)
             Don't I get a watch too?

                                        DISSOLVE TO:

THE ROULETTE TABLE - ONE HOUR LATER

Our trio watch other people playing. Gary turns around and
notices a blackjack table with a note on one of the spaces.
The note says, "reserved". Also, there are several stacks of
chips next to the sign. Gary goes to the dealer.

                         GARY
             Who belongs to this spot?

                         DEALER
             A fine player sir. One of our
             best. He's taking a little break.

Gary throws some chips on an empty spot. Then, he takes a
seat. His fat is not comfortable in this chair.

                         GARY
             I'm in.

Gary throws some chips on his spot. The dealer counts it.

                    DEALER
          I'm sorry sir, but I'm afraid this
          table has a twenty-five-dollar limit.

                     GARY
          No problem.

Gary reaches into his pocket and pulls out a handful of
chips. He bets several chips. The dealer arranges his them.
Then, a waitress comes by and hands Gary a drink. Gary takes
a sip and is in instant heaven. Then, Gary picks up a five-
dollar chip and gives it to the waitress.

                    WAITRESS
          Thank you, Mr. Vitali.

                     GARY
          Just, keep 'em coming.

The waitress moves to the next table. Gary gets twenty-one.

                     GARY
                    (elated)
          I did it again.

The dealer finishes her hand. She pays all the active hands
and pays Gary one and a half times his bet. Then, Gary spots
Henry coming closer. Gary puts his head down. Then, Henry
finds a seat at Gary's table. It's the "reserved" seat.

                 GARY (CONT'D)
                  (to dealer)
          Don't tell me, "he's reserved?".

                    DEALER
          Yes sir. I'm afraid he is.

Henry spots Gary. Jeff and Rick are standing behind Gary.

                    HENRY
          Hi ya men!

                     GARY
          One more, "hi ya men" and I'll
          break off your arm! (a threat) You
          get it?

Gary grabs all his chips and leaves the table.

SHOT ON GARY: HE SEES A FAMILIAR FACE
                    GARY (CONT'D)
          I don't believe it.

                         RICK
                    (nervous)
               Do you see the shooter?

WE PAN GARY - AS HE HEADS INTO A GROUP OF VALETS

Gary's lifelong friend, "Gig" is front of him. They hug.

                         GIG
               It's so good to see. I always see
               your dad and I ask about you.

                         GARY
               I appreciate it. Just seeing you
               brings back so many memories.

                         GIG
               I'm hearing you've got problems.

                         GARY
               How'd you know?

                         GIG
               Valet's know everything.

                         GARY
               In that case, I'll keep moving.

                         GIG
               You still gamble and play slots?

                         GARY
               All the time. Why?

                         GIG
               Well, here's the thing ... in
               this place, there's a foolproof
               way to cheat the slots and win
               jackpots.

                    GARY
          Tell me. What is it? I gotta
          know.
                    GIG
          Well, it works on slots. See,
          every area of the slots has a
          boss. When you find the expensive
          slots, stay there until it gets
          slow. Then, the boss calls in
          a mechanic to set the slot to
          pay off. They put a shill on the
          machine to play and she hits big
          jackpots ... Once she's done,
          the mechanic resets the machine
          again.

                    JEFF
          So we get to it first and we'll
          win.

                    GARY
          Cool.

Gig puts his arm around Gary ...

                    GIG
          Look. I know someone's trying to
          take you out. It's serious shit.

Gig and Gary keep talking. Rick's on to other things.

                    RICK
               (to Jeff)
          Since Gary's busy, why don't we
          hit the buffet.

                    JEFF
          Sounds good to me.

                                    DISSOLVE TO:

INT. PENTHOUSE - HOURS LATER - NIGHT

Rick and Jeff enter. They are burned out.

                         RICK
          Damn! We really won on that slot.

                         JEFF
          Gary's friend was right to a
          "T".

                         RICK
          Those machines are really fixed.

                         JEFF
          Let's wake Gary up and tell him how
          much we won. He'll want his cut.

                                              CUT TO:

INT. GARY'S ROOM - CONTINUING - 6 A.M.

Gary is sprawled across his bed. He's fast asleep. He's only
wearing underwear. His clothes are scattered across his room
like there was an explosion at a clothing store.

Jeff and Rick view all this from the doorway.

                         JEFF
          He could at least cover up.

                         RICK
          Don't wake him. Let's sleep too.

Rick and Jeff exit Gary's room as Gary mumbles to himself.

                                            DISSOLVE TO:

EXT. STRIP - THE NIGHT LIGHTS FADE OUT AS THE SUN COMES UP

INT. PENTHOUSE - CONTINUING - THREE HOURS LATER

Rick enters and crosses into Jeff's room.

INT. JEFF'S ROOM - HE'S ASLEEP.

                         RICK
                    (claps his hands)
          Wake up!

                         JEFF
                    (jumps up)
               What time is it?

                         RICK
               Time to hit the pool.

                         JEFF
               What about Gary? Does he know?

                         RICK
               Let him sleep. He can't stand
               still long enough to get a tan.

                         JEFF
               I know. If he isn't tan in five
               minutes, he gets mad.

Jeff gets out of bed and throws his trunks on. Then, they
walk into the main room. Gary is dressed and awake. He's
dressed as an "Elvis" impersonator. He picks at some left
over food. They head for the door.

                         GARY
               It's about time you guys got up.

                         RICK
               I'm not going downstairs with
               you like that. Don't you have
               something else. Something less
               stupid looking?

They head for the door and close it.

                         GARY
               You know it all burned in the
               fire.

                         JEFF
               People don't walk around like
               that?

                         GARY
               Why not? There's probably at least
               five guys dressed like me, right now.

                    RICK
        Look. We're heading to the pool.
        Come dressed any way you want.

                    JEFF
        Well, I don't like this one bit.

                    RICK
        What do you care, Jeff? He's just
        gonna wander off anyway.

                    JEFF
        Yeah. I forgot it was Gary.

They wait for the elevator. Then, it opens and they enter.

                 JEFF (CONT'D)
        You wanna do a show tonight?

                    RICK
        If Gary's dressing like that
        tonight, we'll be in the show.

                    GARY
        You guys wanna get something to
        eat?

                    RICK
        We can eat by the pool.

                                    DISSOLVE TO:

EXT. POOL AREA - MINUTES LATER

It's very crowded. Almost everyone carries a drink in each
hand. The cabanas are all full of people. But, the entrance
has a velvet belt controlled by two big men.

                  FIRST MAN
        Sorry gentlemen. We're at
        capacity. No more dudes.

                    RICK
        Can't you check your list.

The second man reaches for the list.

                    SECOND MAN
         Name please.

                      RICK
         Vitali, Gary Vitali.

Hearing this, both men can't wait to remove the velvet rope.
The stand even falls over.

                   FIRST MAN
         I'm so sorry Mr. Vitali sir. I'm
         breaking in a new man here.

                      RICK
         Just watch it from now on.

                      JEFF
         Of course, you'll send over your
         finest bottles to our cabana?

                    SECOND MAN
         But, there are no more cabanas.

The first man hits the second man with his hand.

                   FIRST MAN
         Kick somebody out of a cabana!
         I don't care if it's "George
         Clooney."

                    SECOND MAN
         Yes sir. Right away sir.

The second man races past our guys and hurries a group of
people out of their cabana. They are not happy.

                    SECOND MAN
         Here you go, gentlemen. The best
         we have to offer.

Our guys are very pleased as they sit on their loungers.

                 SECOND MAN (CONT'D)
         Drinks will be here in moments.

He hurries off. Rick and Jeff admire all the beautiful girls in and around the pool. Then Gary shows up.

                    GARY
          Sorry I'm late. A couple of babes
          couldn't stop touching me.

                    RICK
          Sure. We thought that would
          happen.

                    JEFF
          Man. This is the life.

                    RICK
          I know. All the women. It's gotta
          be easy to pick up girls.

                    JEFF
          Are you kidding. We look like big
          shots and these cabanas are chick
          magnets. They gotta figure we're
          rich. Present company excepted.

                    GARY
          And what's that supposed-to mean?

Two girls stop by when they see our guys.

                    FIRST GIRL
               (to Rick)
          Are you guys famous?

                    RICK
          Yeah. I'm Brad Pitt and he's
          Ferris Bueller. (indicates Jeff)

                    JEFF
          And I'm sure you know the "King."

The second girl jumps up and down: Gary tries to do his best
Elvis imitation and it works on the girls.

                    SECOND GIRL
          Oh, Elvis. I just love you. Would
          you please sign something for me?

> GARY
>
> Sure, sugar. What should I sign?

The girl pulls down her top and exposes her breasts.

> SECOND GIRL
>
> Our "boobs"

Rick and Jeff's mouths hang open and their eyes pop out of their heads as Gary come up with a pen and signs her breasts. Gary's having a bit of a hard time. They keep jiggling. Rick moves over to assist.

> RICK
>
> I'd better help hold them puppies so the ink doesn't smear.

Rick cups the girl's breasts as Gary signs each one. He signs "Elvis Aaron Presley". Then, the other girls takes her turn. Seeing this, Jeff moves in and bumps Rick away.

> JEFF
>
> I'm the official, official breast holder. That was my major in college.

Jeff holds her breasts while Gary signs again. Once finished, the girls giggle and scamper away.

> GARY
>
> Was that ever cool or what?

> RICK
>
> If I didn't see it with my own eyes, and touch them with my bare hands...

> JEFF
> (interrupting)
> I know, I know. Great nipples.

> RICK
> (to Gary)
> You just keep signing 'em and we'll keep holding them.

                    GARY
          Oh, by the way. I got laid while
          you big shots were sleeping.

                    RICK
          Bull shit!

                    GARY
          I fucked the maid who makes our
          beds.

                    RICK
          I don't believe it.

                    GARY
          Fine. Go check out the stain I
          left.

                    JEFF
          Yuck!!!

Rick hands Gary a drink.

                    RICK
          Have some drinks with us and take
          off your shirt. You might get a
          tan.

Gary takes off his "Elvis" shirt. He takes a couple of sips
of his drink. Then;

                    GARY
                (slurring his words)
          Oh man. I'm drunk. I'm plastered!

                    RICK
          C'mon Gary. You had one sip!

                    GARY
          No. I'm drunk. I really am.

Gary sits down and puts his drink down.

                    GARY (CONT'D)
          I swallowed too much.

                    JEFF
That's what she said.

                    GARY
I see three of you ... Am I tan
yet?

                    RICK
Are you nuts. You don't get a tan
in two seconds and you're not
drunk.

                    JEFF
Nobody gets drunk off of one sip.

                    GARY
I'd better call my dad.

                    RICK
Shouldn't you sober up first?

                    GARY
Oh yeah!

                    JEFF
        (to Rick)
How you doin'. Are you drunk too?

                    RICK
Yeah, right!

Jeff stands up. He's now blocking Rick's view.

                RICK (CONT'D)
I'm glad you're here but, you're
blocking my view.

Rick turns around and sees several girls in bikinis.

                    RICK
I see what you mean.

                    GARY
Yeah, yeah. Me too.

                         JEFF
                    (to Gary}
              Sober up, rummy!

                         GARY
              I think it finally wore off.

                         RICK
              That's good. You shouldn't drink.

                         GARY
              Maybe the sun got me drunk.

                         JEFF
              Maybe.

                         GARY
              Well, how about now. Am I tan
              yet?

                         RICK
              Geeze! It takes time to get a
              tan.

                         GARY
              Then, I'm leaving.

He grabs his shirt and pulls it on. He gets up.

                    GARY (CONT'D)
              Screw this. I'll see you later.

Gary exits the pool area. As he does, several people point
to him and gossip. He's followed by several girls.

                         JEFF
              He really believes he's "Elvis".

Jeff and Rick laugh as Gary walks out of sight.

                                             CUT TO:

INT. JEWERLY STORE-- MINUTES LATER -

Gary walks over to the sunglass case. He spots a pair on a
glittery stand. A woman comes over.

> WOMAN
Those are perfect for you sir.

> GARY
They are?

> WOMAN
Would you believe Mr. Presley
bought some of these very ones
himself?
> GARY
He did? (excited) I'll try 'em
on.

The woman takes them out of the case and hands them to Gary.

Gary puts them on. He looks into a mirror on the case.

> WOMAN
A perfect fit. I must look away.
You look exactly like him.

> GARY
> (excited)
Charge them to my room.

> CUT TO:

INT. CASINO - MINUTES LATER

Gary walk slowly through the casino so that people will see
him. He's wearing his new glasses. He stops at different
games and watches. Then, a strange woman approaches him.

> STRANGER
Do you work here?

> GARY
> (insulted)
No!

> STRANGER
> (disappointed)
What a let down.

He walks away as Rick and Jeff approach.

                    RICK
Where have you been. We've been
looking all over trying to find you.

                    GARY
I've been right here.

                    JEFF
You can't just walk around in
here. You're an easy a target.

                    RICK
There's a bikini contest at the
pool. Maybe you can be a judge.

                    GARY
No thanks. I wanna stay here.
They love me in here.

                    JEFF
Really? If anything, they think
you're an "Elvis impersonator"!

                    GARY
No they don't. They think I'm
really Elvis.

                    JEFF
You idiot! How many times do we
have to tell you that Elvis is
dead.
                    RICK
You can't walk around like this.

                    GARY
I've got it all figured out.
Whoever's trying to kill me is
looking for Gary. And as long
as I continue to be Elvis,
he'll never know it's me. It's
brilliant!!!

                    RICK
That's crazy. You're crazy.

                         GARY
             I'm alive.

                         JEFF
             So far, so good. So far, so good.

Gary pats his chest

                         GARY
             Don't forget my extra protection.

Suddenly, Gary's gun falls to the ground. It fires...

SFX: GUNSHOT

The gun fires a bullet which hits the base of the chandelier
causing it crash down onto a crap table loaded with players.

                       PLAYERS
                     (screaming)

Rick grabs the gun off the floor and rushes Gary away from the
scene. Jeff follows as people in the casino panic.

They stop in the corner by the elevators.

                         RICK
                     (to Gary)
             Are you out of your mind? I'm
             keeping this thing, period!

                         GARY
             Everyone thought it was part of
             the show.

                         RICK
             Are you delusional? What show?
             There was no show!

Jeff comes running over. He has a towel with him. Rick sticks
the gun into the towel and gives it to Jeff.

                         RICK
                     (to Jeff)
             He's not to get this back.

                    JEFF
          It's a good thing that dear old
          dad didn't give Gary a machine
          gun.

                    RICK
          Take it up to the room and hide
          it.

Jeff heads for the elevators.

                    GARY
          What am I supposed to do now?

                    RICK
          Use your mouth. It's you best
          protection.

                    GARY
          Not funny Rick.

                    RICK
          You need to walk around. Just
          walk.

He grabs Gary's arm. They head into the casino. Then, a
little boy comes up to Gary with a pen and a pad of paper.
He holds it up for Gary to take. Gary takes it.

                    BOY
          My grandma would like your
          autograph.

Gary quickly signs it and hands it back to the boy. He runs
to his grandma. She's at least 90. She studies the paper.

                    GRANDMA
               (to herself) (puzzled)
          Who's Gary?

                    GARY
          What do you have to say now? Huh?
          That just proves it. I'm Elvis.

                    RICK
          Like I said before. Elvis has

                    (RICK CONT'D)
been dead for about forty years and
the news probably hasn't caught up
with her yet. (beat) Honestly, I
don't know what kind of thrill you
get pretending to be him.

Jeff returns from upstairs and puts a piece of paper in front
of Gary's face.

                    JEFF
              (altered voice)
     May I please have your autograph?

Gary takes it and signs the paper. He sees Jeff laughing.

                    GARY
     Screw off!

                    RICK
     C'mon Elvis. Let's find one of
     those machines that your friend
     told us about. It really worked
     for us while you slept.

                    GARY
     How great?

                    JEFF
     Over two thousand.

                    RICK
     And before you start bitching and
     moaning, we put your share aside.

                    GARY
     So, I get half, right?

                    JEFF
     Wrong! We all get one third.
     (beat) You know, we could have
     told you we lost.

                    GARY
     But, you didn't. I'm too cleaver:
     or clever.

Rick spots a casino mechanic. He's closing up a slot machine at the end of a row. Rick takes Gary to the machine.

                    RICK
          Let's go.

Just as our trio reaches the machine, Henry beats them to it and drops in a dollar.

                    HENRY
          Sorry. First guy in, owns the
          game.

Henry pulls the lever. (Then) A Jackpot!

SEX: BELLS

                    HENRY (CONT'D)
          You guys are just too slow for
          me.

                    JEFF
               (to Rick)
          What do you say I bring down that
          gun from the room?

Rick, super upset, grabs some of Henry's winnings and fills up a couple of buckets. He shoves the buckets on Henry's lap.

                    RICK
          All right now. You've won your
          money, now hands off our machine!

Henry spots a security guard and motions to him.

                    HENRY
          I wish I could. (BEAT) Hey, I
          know. Why don't we all become
          partners?

                    JEFF
          That's a good idea. Why don't you
          play these next two machines and
          we'll play this one?

                        HENRY
            I don't know. I think I'll ask
            the security guard.

Henry turns around but, the guard has disappeared.

                        HENRY (CONT'D)
                    (laughs nervously)
                    (then, to Gary)
            You know, you look exactly like
            Elvis Presley.

                        GARY
            I know.

Henry drops in another dollar and gets another jackpot.

SFX: BELLS

                        HENRY
            WHOOPEE!!! I won again.

Henry fills up his buckets with more dollars. Rick and Jeff
are ready to pounce on him.

                        GARY
            I gotta go to the room?

                        RICK
            Why?

                        GARY
            I need to piss.

                        JEFF
            What's wrong with the bathrooms
            down here? They're everywhere.

                        GARY
            I can't go down here. They're not
            like room bathrooms.

                        RICK
            What the hell does that mean?

                    GARY
        Hotel guests pee differently in
        their rooms.

                    RICK
        That's the biggest bunch of crap

                    JEFF
        I gotta go too.

                    RICK
                (frustrated)
        What about our machine? You guys
        are screwing up the plan.

Gary walks away, followed by Jeff. Rick shrugs and goes after
them. In the b.g. WE HEAR HENRY

                    HENRY
        <u>Whoo hoo</u>! <u>I hit another</u>
        <u>jackpot</u>!!!

                                        DISSOLVE TO:

INT. MR. VITALI'S OFFICE - CONTINUING

He's sitting at his desk. Sal is sitting on the couch
reading the newspaper. Mr. Vitali's busy on the phone.

                    MR. VITALI
                (into phone)
        Just make sure it gets done!

He slams down the phone. He turns his attention to Sal.

                    MR. VITALI (CONT'D)
        I need you to perform a task for
        me.

He opens his desk and removes a box. He offers it to Sal.

                    MR. VITALI (CONT'D)
        Take it.
Sal takes the box, puts on his hat and leaves the office.

                                        DISSOLVE TO:

INT. PENTHOUSE - LATER THAT NIGHT

Jeff and Rick are sitting around. Gary is still in his room

                    RICK
                (to himself)
          What the hell takes him so long?

Gary enters the room. He's still dressed as Elvis.

                    JEFF
          The least you could do is change

                    GARY
          These are all I have.

                    RICK
          You broke down and bought
          glasses. Why don't you buy some
          jeans?

                    GARY
          Forget it. I like my Elvis stuff.

                    RICK
                (getting up)
          Let's go.

Gary heads for the door. He opens it.

                    GARY
          I just wanna check first.

                    JEFF
          Look who's paranoid.

ANGLE DOWN HALLWAY - A MAN IS SITTING IN A CHAIR AT THE END

INT. DOOR - GARY SLAMS IT SHUT

                    GARY
          We can't go out there!

                    RICK
          Why not?

                    GARY
          A guy's out there. It's him!

                    JEFF
          Are you nuts.

                    RICK
          How the hell do you know?

                    GARY
          Quick Rick. I need the gun.

                    RICK
          Forget it.

Jeff looks out the door and closes it.

                    JEFF
          That guy's probably security.

                    GARY
          If it's him, they'll be no
          witnesses

                    JEFF
          I'm telling you, he's security.

Gary goes to the door and opens it. He walks down the hall.

                    GARY
          I'm gonna talk to this guy.

INT. HALLWAY - CONTINUING

Gary heads towards the man.

                    SAL
          Hi ya kid.

                    GARY
          Don't I know you?

                    SAL
          Yeah. I work for your old man.

                                                        CUT TO:

SERVICE ELEVATOR CLOSE BY - CONTINUING

The doors open and a man exits. Sal is still seated

FULL ANGLE BEHIND GARY AND SAL - The man aims the gun at
Gary. Sal pushes Gary on the floor and draws his gun.

                          SAL
          Get down!

BOTH MEN SHOOT AT EACHOTHER. SAL STANDS.

SFX: GUN SHOTS - MUFFLED BECAUSE EACH GUN HAS A SILENCER.

The man from the elevator shoots Sal in the chest. Then, the
man disappears back into the elevator. Gary tries to take
the gun from Sal. but can't. Sal has a good grip.

                          SAL
          Scram kid! You're the target!

Sal passes out. Gary runs down the hallway.

                                                        CUT TO:

INT. PENTHOUSE - CONTINUING

Gary enters and slams the door. He puts a chair up against
it. He tries to push a table as well, but it's too heavy.

                          RICK
          What's with you?

                          GARY
             (sweating)
          Block the door with this table.

                          JEFF
          What the hell's going on?

                          GARY
          Murder! They just killed Sal!

                         RICK
          Who's Sal?

                         GARY
          I can't say.

                         JEFF
          We didn't hear anything.

                         GARY
          That's cause they used silencers.

                         GARY
          Shut up and see for yourselves.
          I'm calling 911.

                         RICK
          All right already. But, no 911!

Rick opens the door and checks out the hallway - <u>NOBODY</u>

                         GARY
          Is that the first time you ever
          saw a dead guy?

                         RICK
          There's no dead guy. Is he okay?

                         JEFF
          There's no guy?

Gary opens the door and looks out. He quickly closes it.
Gary is completely stunned.

                                        CUT TO:

INT. STAIRWAY - MINUTES LATER

Sal is sitting on the stairs. His jacket's off. He's on his
cell phone.

SFX: A SQUIB EXPLODES ON THE JACKET

It gets gooey stuff on Sal and makes a mess.

                              SAL
                    (on phone)
            It's done sir ... Yep! He's outta
            here.

Sal puts his phone in his pocket and heads down the stairs.

                                          CUT TO:

INT. PENTHOUSE - MOMENTS LATER

                              RICK
            I don't believe any of this.

                              GARY
            Why would I make this up?

                              RICK
            Cause it's you!

Rick opens the door and starts to head out. Jeff follows

                              JEFF
            Are you coming or what?

                              GARY
            Okay. I'll go. But I'm really
            scared

                                          CUT TO:

INT. CASINO - THEY SEE HENRY PLAYING A SLOT AND GO OVER.

                              JEFF
            There's that little bastard!

Our guys stand behind Henry. Henry hits another jackpot.

SFX: BELLS RING - MONEY BEGINS POURING OUT OF THE MACHINE.

                              RICK
            You're done Henry. Cash out!

Gary opens up his jacket and shows Henry his gun.

               HENRY
      Well, why not. I guess I'll go.

Rick immediately takes Henry's seat and puts in some money.
Rick loses hand after hand. This machine's cold. Then,
Gary looks around and sees a casino mechanic working on a
machine. The mechanic finishes and shuts the slot door.

               GARY
      Let's go over there.

Our guys make a mad dash for the machine.

               JEFF
      Who's got some dollars?

Then, Henry enters the scene with buckets full of money.

               HENRY
      I've got lots of them.

Rick stands between Henry and the machine.

               RICK
      This is our machine.

Rick grabs Henry's arm

             RICK (CONT'D)
      Try pulling a lever with a broken
      arm.

               HENRY
      I'll call security.

               JEFF
      Call security if you want. We
      were here first. And that's it!

                                      CUT TO:

A man standing between two machines. He can easily see our
boys. Then, he raises a gun and fires it at Gary.

SFX: GUNSHOT FROM SILENCER

The bucket of coins held by Henry get the bullet and the bucket explodes. Money is all over. A crowd quickly gathers and tries getting the money. Henry waves people away.

                    HENRY
          It' s mine! Mine! Hands off!

Henry looks up at Rick. He expects a little help.

                    HENRY
          Aren' t you gonna help?

Gary primes the slot machine. Rick shakes his head at Henry

                    RICK
          Sure we are. Gary's gonna keep
          the machine warmed up for ya.
          (laughs)
Gary hits a jackpot right-away.

                    GARY
          Whoohoo!!!

                    JEFF
          It's about time. What took so
          long?

                    GARY
          Five hundred bucks, guys.

A change girl comes over as the machine stops.

                    CHANGE GIRL
          You got two hundred from the
          machine. (she gives Gary three
          hundred) And here's three more to
          make five hundred.

Gary drops in a dollar and pulls the lever. Another jackpot

                    GARY
          Only a hundred.

                    RICK
          You gotta put in five coins for the
          big jackpot. (Impatiently) C'mon!

                    CHANGE GIRL
            I might as well stay with you
            guys.

Gary puts in more coins. He pulls the lever.

                    GARY
            Gig should get some of this.

Another jackpot. The dollars start to pour out. The change
girl counts out more money.

                    CHANGE GIRL
            Here's four hundred more. I have
            to leave to get more money.

She walks towards the casino cage. Gary puts more coins in,
but no jackpot. Jeff puts money in and pulls but, no jackpot.
Gary tries again as the Change Girl comes over.

                    CHANGE GIRL
            Any more jackpots?

The wheels on the machine all stop on, "Desert Sands"

SFX BELLS & SIREN

                    CHANGE GIRL (CONT'D)
            You did it guys!

                    GARY
            No I didn't. (beat) What did I
            do?

                    RICK
            You broke the bank! Ten thousand!

The guys all hug.

                    CHANGE GIRL
            Right! You wanna follow me when
            you're done hugging?... I'll
            wait.

She puts an, out of order sign on the machine. Then,
everyone follows her to the cashier.

A cashier approaches them from behind the cage.

                    CHANGE GIRL
          Ten thousand on number 52.

She gives her a slip. Then, the cashier takes out a form and
gives it to Gary. He nervously gives it to Rick

                    GARY
          You fill it out Rick.

                    RICK
          What's the big deal. It just
          wants some basic info and your
          social.

                    GARY
          I don't have a social security
          card.

                    JEFF
          You're kidding? You have to have
          gotten one when you started
          working.

                    GARY
          I know. But, I've never worked. I
          never had a job.

                    RICK
          You're unreal. You're like
          invisible.

A manager sees Gary and comes over.

                    MANAGER
               (to cashier)
          Give Mr. Vitali anything he
          wants.

The manager takes the paper and crumbles it up. Then, he
uses his key and opens the cash drawer.

                    MANAGER
               (to cashier)
          Pay him. Whatever it is.

The cashier counts out $10,000 and gives it to Gary. Rick writes something on a piece of paper and gives it to her.

                              RICK
                  We'd rather have a check please.

Rick takes the money from Gary and gives it to the cashier.

                            CASHIER
                        (looking at paper)
                  Yes sir. Right away.

                                                  CUT TO:

WIDE SHOT - EXT. DESERT SANDS - ENTRANCE AREA

There are several police cars. A handcuffed man is put into one. It's Pauly. On top of the car is a bag containing Pauly's silencer. A cop takes it as he enters the car.

INT. POLICE CAR - CONTINUING

                          VEGAS COP
                  He's a big fish. I wonder who he
                  was after?

                         SECOND COP
                  You know these guys never talk.
                  He'll get bailed out before we
                  can book his gun into evidence.

                          VEGAS COP
                  I know. It's a real pisser.

The Police Car drives off. Lights and siren are on.

                                                  CUT TO:

INT. CASINO CAGE - MINUTES LATER

The cashier returns with a check. She hands it to Gary, but Rick grabs it first.

                            GARY
                  Hey! That's my check.

                    RICK
        It's our check. They need a
        social security number to cash
        it, so I gave 'em mine. My name's
        on it.

                    JEFF
        Let's get back on our machine.

The boys walk through the casino until they get to their
lucky machine. Rick takes the sign off the machine and puts
it into his pocket. He sits down. He rubs his hands together

                    RICK
        Play ball!

Gary drops a dollar into the machine and pulls the lever.
Then, the wheel stop on three bars. Money starts to flow.
Gary fills up another bucket with the money.

                    JEFF
        How much this time?

                    RICK
            (frustrated)
        Only a hundred. (then) Gary,
        what's the matter with you? You
        know we play five at a time. We
        should have hit five times as
        much.

                    GARY
        I thought if we lost, I'd save us
        four dollars.

                    RICK
        Look Einstein. It takes money to
        make money. Always put in the
        maximum amount. Otherwise, you
        might as well play Keno.

                    JEFF
        This has got to be the luckiest
        trip. What do you say, we do
        something else when we're done?

Rick hops off the stool and puts the "out of order" sign back on the machine.

                    RICK
          Why not. No one's gonna touch it.

ANGLE ON ANOTHER MAN HOLDING A GUN BETWEEN MACHINES

CLOSE SHOT ON GUN AS HE PULLS THE TRIGGER - IT FIRES

SFX: GUNSHOT

WE SEE that the "out of order" sign on the machine is hit by the bullet. The force of the blast makes the wheels on the slot machine spin. It stops on a jackpot. Then, money pours out of the machine attracting a crowd. Our boys are headed away totally unaware of what's transpired. They finally reach the cashier. They put three buckets on the counter.

                    JEFF
          These things are heavy.

The cashier takes the buckets and pours them into a counter. When finished, she counts out their money.

                    CASHIER
          Five hundred and forty dollars

Jeff takes the money as Gary also reaches, for it.

                    JEFF
          You gotta be faster than that.

                    GARY
          Asshole!

                    RICK
          Don't get pissed. The money
          belongs to all of us, remember?

                    GARY
          Oh yeah. But I need to hold it.

Then, the guys notice a lot of commotion in the area of their machine. People are still fighting for the money on the floor. Gary starts to go but, Rick pulls him back.

                    RICK
          Who cares what they're doing.
          Here. You hold the money.

Rick hands their latest winnings to Gary. He's pleased.

                    JEFF
          Rick. Try another shot at
          blackjack. (then) Look! There's
          an open seat at that table.

Rick races over to vacant chair and sits down. Jeff is right
behind him. Then, Rick reaches into his pockets and pulls
out a huge bunch of chips in all colors. He puts a $500 chip
on two open spots. Then, he assorts his chips.

                    DEALER
               (to pit boss)
          Blacks in play.

Hearing this, the pit boss comes over to watch.

                    JEFF
          How long are you gonna play?

                    RICK
          I just sat down. Cool your jets
          man

The dealer deals Rick a pair of twos and a pair of threes.
The dealer shows a Jack for the face-up card. Rick's pissed.

                    JEFF
          You know you can surrender your
          hand and only lose half.

                    RICK
          Shut up JEFF. I've just started.

Gary comes back from wherever he was. He's excited.

                    JEFF
          Rick's got a thousand bucks bet.

                    GARY
          Yeah, well, I just signed three

                (GARY CONT'D)
autographs. And on big boobs too.

                     RICK
Shut up you guys. I'm
concentrating

                     JEFF
Yeah, Elvis! Shut the hell up.
And don't bother Rick.

Rick splits his threes and his twos. He now has four hands.

                     RICK
              (excited)
Here we go. I'm splitting.

Rick puts another five hundred on each hand. Then, he's dealt
a third three and a third two.

A cocktail waitress comes over to the table.

              COCKTAIL WAITRESS
Cocktails.

                     JEFF
Go away lady. Come back later.

She looks at the pit boss. He motions for her to leave.

                     RICK
I'm splitting again.

Rick puts another five hundred chip on each new hand. All the
other players put their chips on their cards and wave the
dealer off. They're satisfied with their hands.

            MAN TO RICK'S RIGHT
Good luck man.

                     RICK
Thanks. I think I need a drink.

A crowd has gathered to watch, along with a second pit boss.
Then, Rick waves his hand over all six of his hands.

                    RICK (CONT'D)
          Good. I'm good. But not really!

                    GARY
          Hey! I just remembered a joke.

                    RICK
          Would you shut the hell up!!!
          (then) C'mon dealer.

The dealer pulls out a forth three and a forth two. Rick
covers his face with both hands. He looks at the dealer.
Then, he adds another five hundred chip to both new hands.

                    GARY
          Do you know you've got $8,000
          bet?

Rick turns to Jeff.
                    RICK
          Get him the hell away from me!

                    GARY
          Sorry Rick. I'll shut up.

                    JEFF
          You better. He's gotta
          concentrate.

                    RICK
          I need to think this one out.

Rick moves his chair back a few inches. Gary Jumps back.

                    RICK (CONT'D)
          All right. Let's go dealer. Deal
          'em out. C'mon, be good to me.

Rick gets a <u>King</u>. He quickly decides what to do.

                    RICK (CONT'D)
          I'm staying ... Next hand.

                    DEALER
          I'm sorry, but you have to wave your
          hand if you stay or want a card.

                    RICK
              (waving hand over cards)
         Fine! I'm good.

                    JEFF
         Don't worry. The next cards will
         be better.

The dealer adds a <u>Queen.</u> Rick waves his hand over this cards

                    RICK
         Shut up Jeff. No more words of
         encouragement.

Now, he's dealt a Jack. He says nothing and waves his hand
over the Jack and two. His forth card is a Ten. He waves his
hand over this hand as well. Rick moves his chair back and
stands up. Then he addresses anyone who cares to listen.

                    RICK (CONT'D)
         This is great! So far, I've
         got four thousand bet on King,
         Queen, Jack, and Ten. I should be
         playing frigging' poker.

The crowd nervously laughs for him as a waitress walks by.
She is carrying a tray of drinks. Rick grabs a drink off
her tray and gulps it down. He makes a face as if he drank
gasoline. He throws a chip on her tray.

                    RICK (CONT'D)
              (to waitress)
         What the hell was that?

                    WAITRESS
         It's V.O. sir. (beat) Whiskey.

                    RICK
         It's terrible! Shit!... It might
         as well be a glass of B.O.! Now
         I know I'm in trouble with these
         cards.

Rick sits back down. Gary and Jeff pat Rick's back.

                         JEFF
                  (confidently}
            Don't worry man. You'll win.

                         RICK
            Okay dealer. What do you have for
            this three?

The dealer hits Rick with a <u>Ten</u> and he waves his hand over
it. His next two cards are <u>Queens</u> and he also waves his hand
over them. Then, he is dealt a <u>King</u>. He picks it up along
with his three. He's thinking about his next move.

                    RICK (CONT'D)
                  (disgusted)
            Now I know how he Captain of the
            Titanic felt when he hit the
            iceberg.

Then, out of nowhere, Henry approaches. And, before anyone
can stop him, he gets next to Rick and taps his shoulder.

                         HENRY
            Hi ya, winner! You wanna be
            partners with me on some Keno?

                        DEALER
            Would you like another card?

With his cards in hand, Rick takes a swipe at Henry. He
doesn't realize that his cards are in his hand and the
dealer is going to give him another card. HOUSE RULES: He's
asking for a hit and gets one. He gets a nine and loses.

                         RICK
            Get the hell away from me!

The security guards grab Henry and escort him away as the
dealer takes away Rick's bet of $1,000.

                        DEALER
            I'll need your cards sir.

                         RICK
                  (confused)
            Why? What are you talking about?

                         DEALER
              You busted. You went
              over.

Rick sets his cards down and the dealer takes them. Henry
manages to break away from the guards.

                         HENRY
                    (protesting)
              You can't do this to me. I'm
              a big shot around here. Ask
              "Elvis"!

The guards look over at Gary who happens to be signing a
girl's "boob".

                         GUARD
              I don't think Elvis
              wishes to be bothered.

                                                    CUT TO:

BLACKJACK TABLE - CONTINUING

Rick is upset that the dealer gave him an unwanted card.

                         RICK
                    (to pit boss)
              I didn't want another card! I
              swear. You were watching! I
              stayed on seven crappy hands.
              (beat) Why on earth would I hit
              on the eighth one?

                         PIT BOSS
              Sorry sir, but you did hit it.

                         RICK
              And just when did I do that?

                         PIT BOSS
              You swiped your hand when the
              dealer asked if you wanted
              another card.

                    RICK
        But, I didn't hit! I just turned
        my body. Your security is
        supposed to keep those crazies
        away from me.

                    PIT BOSS
        I'm sorry sir. The video's been
        checked and you did ask for a
        card.

Gary comes over to Rick.

                    GARY
        What's going on Rick?
        Did we win?

                    RICK
                (enraged)
        We? You fucking asshole. No, We
        didn't win. And while you were
        writing on a bunch of "tits",
        that little turd Henry cost me a
        thousand bucks. I ought to turn
        you and Henry into "The Blue Man
        Group"!

                    PIT BOSS
                (to Rick)
        Excuse me sir, but we have to
        finish this hand. Everyone's
        waiting.

The dealer gets ready reveal the face down card.

                    RICK
                (to dealer)
        Fine! Show us a bust card.

The dealer shows a two. The dealer has twelve. Rick's
nervous

                    RICK
        Shit!!! I've got all the tens.

                    GARY
          Maybe if there's no more tens,
          the dealer will get a nine.

                    RICK
               (enraged)
          Are you fucking nuts. If she
          gets a nine, we all lose. That's
          twenty-one

Gary quickly steps back as the dealer shows a King for a
total of twenty-two. Everyone wins. However, Rick doesn't
know this. He's really just pissed at Gary. Everyone cheers
for Rick.

                    RICK
          Come here you. I'm gonna pop your
          head like a grape.

                    JEFF
               (excited)
          You won Rick. Seven thousand
          bucks. You won. Forget Gary.

Everyone at the table is being paid for winning.

                    DEALER
               (to Rick)
          Congratulations sir. Well played.

                    RICK
          I won? (then) (elated) I won!!!

Rick gets out of his chair and grabs Gary as Jeff pats him on
the back.

                    GARY
               (scared)
          Don't touch me man. I know
          karate.

Rick kisses Gary on the cheek. Gary's confused.

                    JEFF
               (to Gary)
          He won, man. He won! We all won.

                    GARY
              (relieved)
         Whoopee!!!

Rick sits back in his chair. He gathers all his chips.

                    DEALER
         Are you in this hand sir?

                    RICK
              (grateful)
         No thanks. I'm finished.

Rick fills up his pockets with his winnings.

                    JEFF
         I hate to admit it, but Henry
         made you hit and that took the
         winning card away from the
         dealer.

                    RICK
         So, what happened to that pest?

                    JEFF
         Security took him away.

                    RICK
         Good. He caused me enough grief.

The guys head for the cashier with all their chips.

                    JEFF
         What do you say we reward
         ourselves with a bunch of naked
         women?

Rick and Jeff put all their chips on the counter and the
cashier begins counting and stacking. Rick looks around.

                    RICK
         Where's Gary?

                    JEFF
         He like disappeared or something.

They take a few steps away to look for Gary and then go back

                    RICK
          I don't know either. (worried)
          Let's get our money and find him.
          Or not!

The cage manager approaches with their strong box. Rick
takes it and uses his key to open it. The cashier gives it
to Rick.

                    CASHIER
          Here you go sir. Good luck.

Rick takes the cash and some chips and put them into the
box. It's almost full. Then, he closes it up and locks it.

                    JEFF
          Do you have any idea how much?

                    RICK
          Nope! And that's what makes this
          such a great trip. Except for
          Gary

                    JEFF
          We still need to find him.

                    RICK
          Right! But you're ruining my
          high!

                                        CUT TO:

INT. HOTEL - HALLWAY OF SHOPS - CONTINUING

Rick and Jeff walk down the hall looking into the shops

EXT. BARBER SHOP

Jeff and Rick pass by and see that Gary's in a chair with a
towel covering his face. They are approached by the barber
as they enter. Rick gives the barber a black chip ($100)

                    RICK
              (whispering)
          Get lost for ten minutes.

The barber picks up a magazine and goes into the back room.
Then, Jeff takes a fresh hot towel and replaces the one on
Gary's face. It's super-hot. Gary instantly reacts in pain

                    GARY
          YEOOW!!!

Gary takes the towel off and sees that his friends laughing

                    GARY (CONT'D)
          Assholes!

                    RICK
          You should have seen your face

Jeff picks off a piece of fringe from Gary's jacket.

                    JEFF
          Don't you think this jacket needs
          some attention?

                    GARY (PISSED)
          It's fine!

                    JEFF
          Hey Rick. Don't you think it's
          time for Elvis to buy some real
          clothes?

                    GARY
          My Elvis clothes are fine. I'm
          still signing autographs aren't
          I?

                    RICK
          You're starting to look a little
          flea-bitten.

                    JEFF
          I'd say a-lot flea-bitten.

Gary takes a fresh hot towel and throws it at Jeff's face

                    GARY
          So does your face.

                    JEFF
          Good comeback Gary. Let's get the
          hell out of here.

Gary takes off his barber gown and throws it on the chair.
He's the first to leave followed by Rick and Jeff.

                    RICK
          Where to now?

                    GARY
          I've gotta go somewhere fast.

                    RICK
          Now another secret meeting

                    JEFF
          He's going to the room to jerk
          off.

                    GARY
              (disgusted)
          Always with the fuckin' comments.

                    JEFF
          Well, they' re better than your
          jokes. At least it's funny.

                    GARY
          I'm laughing hysterically inside.
          See ya.

Gary heads down the hallway. Rick and Jeff follow.

                    RICK
          Come here for a second.

Gary stops and meets up with them.

                    GARY
          Okay. What?

                    JEFF
          Do you know the difference between
          parsley and pussy?

                    GARY
          No. What?

                    JEFF
          No one eats parsley.

Rick and Jeff start laughing. Gary doesn't get it.

                    GARY
          Look you guys. This is really
          serious. I've got to do something
          and when I say it's time to go,
          we go. (beat) I mean it. All
          right?

                    JEFF
          Whatever man. Just watch
          yourself.

Gary is satisfied and walks away from them.

                    RICK
          Whatever he's up to, he's gonna
          get into some kind of trouble.

                                        CUT TO:

INT. DESERT SANDS HALLWAY - DOORS TO CONFERENCE ROOM

Gary enters an empty room. Then, he sees a note and some
keys on the table. The note reads: "Your new car, Love Dad.
Leave Town Now!"

                                        DISSOLVE TO:

EXT. DESERT HIGHWAY - TWO HOURS LATER

INT. GARY' S NEW CAR

Gary's driving a new Honda. Rick is in front. Jeff's in back

                    RICK
You know Gary, we didn't have to
split so fast.

                    JEFF
I still wanted to gamble and
fuck!

                    GARY
You guys owe me a lot. I made you
big winners and I do mean, "BIG"!

                    RICK
Okay, you're a great guy. But
where'd this new car come from?

                    GARY
My dad took care of it.

                    JEFF
Gotta love your dad.

                    GARY
Yep! You sure do.
          (thinking)
You really do.

GARY'S CAR SPEEDS DOWN THE HIGHWAY AND PASSES A FEW CARS.

                 GARY (CONT'D)
Only ten miles to the giant
thermometer. You guys wanna stop?

                    RICK
You burned it the "fuck" down!

                    GARY
Oh yeah. Okay. Let's skip it.

Gary laughs as Jeff leans forward.

                    JEFF
Hey dude. What's the hurry? We
don't want to attract attention.
Especially around here.

SFX: POLICE SIREN

                                                    CUT TO:

HIGHWAY SHOT - GARY'S HONDA IS BEING FOLLOWED BY BLACK AND
WHITE CHP CRUISER. THEN, BOTH CARS PULL OVER.

INT. HONDA

                        GARY
            I should have out-run him.

                        RICK
            Are you nuts? A Honda can't out-
            run a cop car. But what the hell.
            ·When he gets up to the window
            ... floor it to the border. We'll
            find a spot in the desert and lose
            him.

                        GARY
            What do you think Jeff?

                        JEFF
            Are you fuckin' nuts? Rick's
            joking!

WIDE SHOT ON HONDA - TWO COPS APPROACH WITH FLASHLIGHTS ON.
ONE COP IS ON EACH SIDE. THEY SCAN RICK, JEFF AND GARY.

INT. HONDA - CONTINUING

                        GARY
                    (whispering)
            Doesn't that guy look familiar?

CLOSE SHOT OF GAS PEDAL - GARY'S FLOORS IT.

EXTREME WIDE SHOT: THE HONDA LEAVES THE SCENE AS THE COPS
HEAD FOR THEIR CAR

                                                DISSOLVE TO:

EXT. LAS VEGAS COUNTY JAIL - ONE HOUR LATER

SHOOT THRU TO - JAIL HOLDING CELL

Our trio share a bench built for two as several men walk by.

                    JEFF
          (to Gary)
     Any more bright ideas?

                    GARY
     At least my dad knows we're here.

                    RICK
     Those cops were cool. We're not
     even here for speeding away. It's
     all that shit Gary stole from the
     room. He grabbed the whole room.

                    JEFF
     I hate to say it but, this looks
     like a job for the "Mafia".

                    GARY
     Screw you Jeff! I told you that in
     confidence.

                    RICK
     Why the hell did you steal two
     big screens and five bathrobes?

                    GARY
     I thought you wanted some
     souvenirs.

                    RICK
     Well yeah. But, not grand theft
     souvenirs.

                    GARY
     They should be arresting those
     stupid valets. They let us have
     it.

                    JEFF
     Why is nothing ever your fault.
     Huh, Gary?

                    GARY
     It's not my fault. They did it

                    (GARY CONT'D)
because they really thought I
was "Elvis". He's really big in
Mexico.

                    RICK
Again with the Elvis shit. Look
Gary. The only person who thinks
you look like Elvis is you. Get
it? You!

                    JEFF
Don't forget people drunk off
their ass. And I swear to God
that if we ever get home, I'm
gonna burn all your Elvis shit. I
don't even care if you're wearing
it. It's gonna burn!

                    RICK
And, I'm gonna help him.

A jailer opens the cell door. He points at our boys.

                    JAILER
Okay, you three. Up and out. Your
bail's been posted. Let's go!

Our guys look at each other in disbelief. Rick shrugs.

                                        DISSOLVE TO:

EXT. LAS VEGAS JAIL - ALONGSIDE THE STREET - MINUTES LATER

                    RICK
This is too much man. I figured
we'd be stuck in there awhile.

                    JEFF
Why do you think the charges got
dropped?

                    RICK
Who the hell cares. As long as
were out, I don't care how.

                         GARY
                    (agreeing)
          I know. We really got lucky.

                         RICK
          Now, listen to me Gary and listen
          good. If I ever hear the word
          "Elvis" in my presence, I'm going
          to come after you. You get that?

                         GARY
          I don't know why you're mad.

                         JEFF
          It's getting really cold out
          here. Where's the car? I wish
          they'd bring us the car already.

SFX: SCREECHING TIRES

The Honda comes racing around the corner and stops in front
of our trio. The tinted windows keep us from seeing in. Rick
tries to open the door, but it's locked.

SFX: HONKING HORN

Our guys go over to the drivers side. Then, the window
slightly goes down until we notice that it's "Henry"!!!

                         HENRY
                    (slyly)
          Hi ya men! (beat) Didn't expect
          to see me again, did you?

                         GARY
          You?? What the hell's going on?

                         RICK
          Get out of our car!

                         HENRY
          Apparently, you idiots don't follow
          things too well. Listen you mutts. I
          work for Gary's dad. Mr. Vitali. And
          guess what? We're gangsters! Real
          mobsters, just like the movies.

                    GARY
Can I have my car now? It's cold.

                    HENRY
You caught a break kid. You
were born under a lucky star or
something

                    RICK
I don't get it. You were
everywhere we went.

                    JEFF
You kept pissing on our trip.

                    HENRY
Mr. Vitali ordered me to keep an
eye on Gary and that's exactly
what I did. Where ever he went, I
went. And it paid off pretty good
too.

                    GARY
I wanna talk to my dad.

                    HENRY
Not possible, kid.

                    GARY
          (demanding}
Then, get the fuck out of my car!

                    HENRY
          (not phased)
Nope! It's my car now. And, oh
yeah. There's some Highway Patrol
guys inside looking for three
guys who blew up two cars and did
some other shit. I hear they' re
looking to stick a thermometer up
someone's ass. (beat) Know what I
mean???

                    GARY
Well, what are we supposed to do?

Henry smiles as the window starts going up.

                    HENRY
          So long men.

WIDE: THE CAR SPEEDS AWAY LEAVING OUR TRIO ON THE SIDEWALK.

PAN: THE STREETS ARE EMPTY EXCEPT FOR OUR GUYS

CLOSE UP: ON GARY

                    GARY
          You know, (beat) I just thought
          of a funny joke ...

AERIAL SHOT: JEFF WALKS ONE WAY IN ONE DIRECTION AND RICK
WALKS IN ANOTHER.

                    GARY (CONT'D)
          Well, don't you want to hear it?
          It's really funny.

Jeff and Rick keep walking in opposite directions.

                                        FADE OUT:

                    THE END

                    BOUND 4 VEGAS

written by Ron Sellz
WGAw ®

ABOUT THE AUTHOR

When Ron was at Hanna-Barbera studios, he was the writer for Scooby-Doo, as well as The Smurfs, the Snorks and other well known cartoon shows. He also worked on Mork and Mindy and The Pink Panther where he made his reputation! Norman Lear›s production company put Ron to work on Good Times, The Jefferson's, All in the Family and Chips.

Danny Simon, the brother of Neil Simon later brought Ron onto his staff to write for his ABC Special. Neil Simon reportedly always said that it was his brother that taught him to write.

During his free time from all the busy creations that he worked on in Hollywood, Ron took the time to write the Thriller movie called Terror in Paradise. It is still available on Amazon. Also available on DaDons's Rare Laser Discs website and eBay.

Ron often talks about Bud Abbott from the team of Abbott and Costello. When Ron was 16 years old and living in Encino, California, he struck up a friendship with Abbott as he sat at the feet of the master, both as a friend and as a student of comedy writing.

Ron also worked with Sherwood Schwartz, the great writer and producer, over the years. With Sherwood, Ron worked on the Gilligan's Island series for Metro Media. Ron said that each day was so very exciting for him as he watched the characters delivering his written lines for them.

Ron's beloved characters were Gilligan, The Skipper, Mary Ann, Mrs. Howell and the Professor. Two of Ron's favorite stories include his interaction with John Travolta and Wayne Newton.

Hollywood Friends can be found on www.lostagepublishing.com. Ron is also the author of two other books, Pickled, and Bound 4 Vegas.

Ron Sellz resides in Chatsworth, CA, is happily married to his wife Teri, and has three sons: Stuart, Scott and Brandon.

www.ingramcontent.com/pod-product-compliance
Lightning Source LLC
Chambersburg PA
CBHW020645250626
47154CB00008B/2820